THE CURSE OF THE
GIANT HOGWEED

THE CURSE OF THE GIANT HOGWEED

CHARLOTTE MACLEOD

PUBLISHED FOR THE CRIME CLUB BY
DOUBLEDAY & COMPANY, INC.
GARDEN CITY, NEW YORK
1985

FOR ROBERT JOHN GUTTKE
Griffin-Maker to the
Court of King Sfyn

Any resemblance between historical fact and the characters, language, manners, or events in this book would be remarkable to the point of incredulity. The story is purely the result of an enchantment under which the author fell upon visiting the ever-entrancing principality of Wales.

Library of Congress Cataloging in Publication Data
MacLeod, Charlotte.
The curse of the giant hogweed.
I. Title.
PS3563.A31865C8   1985   813'.54
ISBN 0-385-19609-1
Library of Congress Catalog Card Number 84-13578

THE CURSE OF THE
GIANT HOGWEED

CHAPTER 1

"For God's sake, Pete, is that old coot still blethering?"

Professor Timothy Ames was sorry he'd bothered to wake up. He was also sorry he'd fallen asleep. These green fiber glass chairs were hell on an old man's skinny backside. What the Christ were they here for, anyway? He hated being lectured at. He wasn't used to assembly rooms carved willy-nilly out of erstwhile stately homes. He wished he were back at Balaclava Agricultural College in the hinterlands of Massachusetts, U.S.A., checking the boron in the beet fields.

His companion, the if possible even more distinguished Professor Peter Shandy, wished Tim would quit turning off his hearing aid. When it wasn't operating, Tim never knew whether he was mouthing words without letting any sound come out, or bellowing like a bull in rut. This time, Tim had bellowed. Peter could only be thankful they were at a British university, where it seemed not the done thing to notice eccentric behavior in elderly academics.

Perhaps the speaker had his own hearing aid turned off. Despite Tim's outcry and the few muttered "Hear, hears" that had followed it, Peter couldn't see that Professor Pfylltrydd was showing any sign of shutting up. So far Pfylltrydd had said nothing about the giant hogweed, or *Heracleum mantegazzianum*, that the overseas visitors didn't already know.

Naturally Tim and Peter had done their research before they'd agreed to come here and lend their expertise toward eradicating the oversized pest. They'd heard how this gargantuan relative of the cow parsley and the water hemlock was taking over the riverbanks and hedgerows. Smaller plants that couldn't grow in its noxious shade were threatened with extinction. Bird watchers were being carted off to the hospitals with severe cases of whiplash from craning their necks to hurl anathemas up its fifteen-foot stalks. Courting couples were getting contact dermatitis in embarrassing places from brushing against its venomous bristles. Nudist camps were all but wiped out.

Fishermen were succumbing to apoplexy in droves. The accursed weed grew so thick around the streams that they couldn't indulge in their piscatorial pursuits without importing machetes or sharpening up their ancestral broadaxes to hack their way to the water. And the dingy white flower heads were alleged to produce five thousand seeds apiece.

Peter Shandy intended to count a few headfuls of seeds. He was curious to know whether five thousand was a true figure or merely one plucked from the air by some sensation-mongering journalist. The chances were it was fairly close to the mark, though: Mother Nature was apt to err on the side of prodigality.

When it came to wordiness, Professor Pfylltrydd was also a child of nature, that was plain. He was talking about the excellent work already done by hogweed experts on this side of the water. They'd thought for a time they had the hogweed hogtied, but all of a sudden, the weeds had begun to spring new-bristled, taller, ranker, smellier, and more pestiferous than ever before. They'd spread almost overnight to places where no hogweed had previously infiltrated.

This meeting was being held in one such place, among the lush green hills where England blends so delightfully into Wales and the sheep all begin bleating in Cymric as soon as you cross the border. Peter thought he could hear sheep bleating now. Or was that still the old goat maundering on about the hogweed?

Tim was asleep again. Peter was feeling his jet lag. When this ordeal by windbag was over, would his hosts offer him and his companions yet more cups of milky tea, or free them to go somewhere and sink their nozzles into pints of the magnificent local bitter? Peter thought wistfully of the pub in which his wife Helen and her dear friend Iduna Stott were no doubt resting their weary feet and wetting their dainty whistles after an arduous round of the sights and the shops.

It had been understood that he, Tim, and Dan Stott, the third member of their team, wouldn't be able to spend much time with the women. Their hosts were paying Tim's and Peter's expenses, hoping for great results from the developers of such horticultural wonders as *Brassica napobrassica balaclaviensis* and Portulaca Purple Passion. Since he was here on business, he ought to be keeping his mind on the discourse; but it kept drifting off into reveries about the respective excellences of Helen and British beer.

Then Peter sat up with a jolt. The speaker had actually and finally stopped speaking. There was a spattering of applause in which he only just managed to join. The learned lady conducting the seminar, whose name Peter couldn't for the life of him recall, was now suggesting their distinquished guest Professor Ames, or perhaps Professor Stott, or even Professor Shandy would care to address some of the points Professor Pfylltrydd had just raised.

Tim didn't stir. Dan Stott, on Peter's other side, was sitting rapt in reverie, perhaps computing the number of hogs that might be needed to eat up all those acres of hogweed, and wondering what would be the effects on their digestive systems if they tried. Obviously, it was up to Shandy.

Peter couldn't remember any questions other than Tim's which had been brought up by Professor Pfylltrydd's discourse, so he decided to go with that one. He detached himself from his abominable chair, sauntered up to the front of the room wearing the expression of mixed humility and conscious self-satisfaction deemed appropriate for such occasions, took hold of the sides of the lectern, smiled (not broadly but enough to show he wasn't actually hostile), and said his piece.

"I expect you'll all agree that my learned colleague, if I may presume to call him so, has given us sufficient—er—food for thought at this juncture. Rather than take up your time with speculations on what might or might not be feasible courses of action, I'm simply going to ask that you point Professor Ames, Professor Stott, and myself in the general direction of a reliable car hire agency, a decent pub, and a clump of giant hogweed. Once we've done a little fieldwork, I trust it won't be long before we come up with some recommendations."

"On what do you base this confident expectation of a speedy result?" demanded the inevitable cynic in the back row.

Timothy Ames was awake now. He heard that one perfectly, and was ready with the answer.

"On the fact that Professor Shandy's wife has spent half the winter writing a paper on Belial Buggins, the Bard of Balaclava. She's been asked to present it at a conference in Arizona next month and there'll be hell to pay if we don't finish here in time to get her back for the presentation. Any further questions?"

There were none. Several of the listening savants smiled, one or two laughed aloud, and a learned academic discussion broke out as to which pub had the best bitter. The meeting was adjourned to the Pig in Clover. Peter had a pint and a plowman's lunch. Tim had a half and a small wedge of poacher's pie. Dan had the rest of the pie, a few pasties, and two pints. On their way to the car hire, he purchased five punnets of gooseberries and a whole Cheddar cheese to tide them over until they could get to a proper restaurant.

Peter had intended to rent a big car—big at least by United Kingdom standards—but there were only Fiats available. That was all right, they'd manage. Aside from their field equipment, he and the boys had little luggage. Peter himself carried his grandfather Shandy's old black cowhide satchel with a change of underwear, his razor, and field clothes to replace the good gray suit and white shirt he'd worn to the lecture. Tim had a clean pair of socks and a spare battery for his hearing aid crammed into a pocket of his hairy old brown tweed jacket. Dan had his cheese, his gooseberries, and a pigskin suitcase packed with God knew what—sandwiches, probably—by the loving hands of Iduna. Dan got in back with the impedimenta, Tim climbed in front on the passenger's side, and Peter got to drive.

He'd expected that; in fact, he'd have insisted on driving. Peter was not only the youngest of the three, he was also the most likely to stay awake, to recall where they were going, to keep on the left-hand side of the road, and to know a giant hogweed when he saw one.

Once they'd found a suitable place to start, he and Tim would begin collecting plant specimens and soil samples. Dan Stott's function, as head of Balaclava's animal husbandry department and a noted authority on swine culture, was more nebulous. Peter suspected Dan had invited himself and Iduna along mainly because he found something appealing in the mere concept of a giant hogweed, and might secretly be on the side of the enemy. Dan would bear watching. That shouldn't be hard, of course, Stott's dimensions being what they were.

Whatever might be in store for them, the three old friends were merry enough as they set off on their quest for the giant hogweed. Nor were they long in finding some. It would have been difficult not to. The hedgerows so sensibly allowed over here to grow up and provide natural fences, refuges for small wildlife, and antierosion barriers for the soil instead of being mowed flat in the alleged interest of modern efficiency, were being taken over by the biggest and ugliest representative of the Umbelliferae.

The band of hogweed-hunters didn't stop to examine any of the available specimens though, until they'd put a safe distance between themselves and the halls of academe. The woods, as Tim observed darkly, might be full of goddamn professors wanting to make speeches. They couldn't be too careful. Hence it was not until the Fiat had carried them well into Wales that Dan Stott, who had steeled himself not to emit grunts of anguish at each pub they passed, suggested they might now think of stopping for refreshment.

Peter didn't mind. The field behind the pub toward which Dan pointed was rife with some of the tallest and thickest hogweed they'd spotted thus far.

Tim was all for stopping, too. "At least they'll have a gents", he observed. "One thing about the British. And the Welsh, I suppose I'd better say before they run me out of the country. They've got a civilized attitude toward the natural functions."

The pub even had a parking lot, about ten feet square and

surrounded by a high stone wall. Peter couldn't get the Fiat in, though, until a brewer's lorry had accomplished the patently impossible feat of making a full turn, then squeezing through a gateway some four inches narrower than the lorry. This being the land of Merlin, it took the driver three minutes. After that, they had the lot to themselves. Peter pulled up next to a rear door that led directly to the necessary offices. Dan, who'd finished the gooseberries but brought his cheese along for company, went with Tim into the men's room. Peter went on ahead to the bar.

As so often happens in country pubs, he found the room empty. That was all right. Peter didn't mind standing there admiring the mellow patina on the polished brass pump handles, weighing the relative merits of ale and lager. This place had an odd sort of atmosphere about it, he thought, and tried to figure out why. Perhaps it was simply that nobody was here, neither behind the bar nor hunched on one of the benches behind a pint glass as tall as his head. Perhaps it was because the pub was old. Really old, not tarted-up old.

To be sure, in this area anything not built by Edward the Second might be considered relatively modern. This had been a public house well before Edward's time, though. Maybe long before. Peter Shandy couldn't have said how he knew. The pub was clean enough, and reasonably well kept up. It must have been renovated many times. Nevertheless it smelled old. No, more than old. Primeval, like a forest floor that had never been cleared and put to the plow.

In centuries gone they'd brewed their own beer here, no doubt. It would have been thick and heavy, served in leather jacks that never got washed between one customer and the next. The customers wouldn't have been washed, either. They'd have had on crude homespun or leather garments, stiffened with sweat to the shapes of their bodies. The pub wouldn't have smelled old then. It would have stunk like a pigsty.

Not one of Dan Stott's pigsties, of course. Dan held to the tenet that a clean pig was a happy pig. No doubt he knew whereof he mucked; at least Dan's pigs always appeared happy enough. What the hell was keeping Dan, anyway? Where was Tim? Where was the publican? Where was anybody?

Great balls of fire, where was Peter Shandy? Gradually, without his knowing when or how, Peter's feet had moved from ancient oak planking to forest floor. This had never, not possibly, been anything other than forest floor. The trees around him had roots as big around as beer kegs, knotted into the earth like giant hawsers, as they needs must be to hold upright the incredible trunks growing from them.

There was a simple explanation for this phenomenon, Peter thought. He was drunk. No, that wouldn't work. He still hadn't laid eyes on the bartender, let alone got his pint. He'd fallen asleep, that was it. He'd succumbed to jet lag and the backlash from Professor Pfylltrydd's learned discourse. Or maybe he'd hypnotized himself staring at those shiny pump handles.

No matter. Tim and Dan would come along and rouse him as soon as they'd finished whatever was taking them so long back there. In the meantime, he might as well relax and enjoy his nap.

It felt strange to know he was asleep, yet not feel the least bit sleepy. But then one usually didn't, in a dream. One didn't always have such powerful tactile sensations, either. Peter slapped at a gnat that was lunching on his cheekbone, and made blasphemous utterance as he banged his toe on one of those mammoth tree roots.

It was odd that his toe hurt from the banging, come to think of it. He'd put on his heavy work boots when they'd got into the Fiat. Peter looked down at his feet and saw he was wearing primitive buskins made of roughly shaped leather drawn up over his feet like the dough around an apple in a dumpling. Thongs were laced across the tops and around his ankles to keep them on.

Well, such things happened in dreams. He ought to be grateful he was having this relatively innocuous excursion around the fringes of the subconscious instead of the recurring nightmare in which he'd find himself lecturing to a crowded classroom, stark naked except for a giant hogweed stuck Hawaiian-style behind his right ear. Or was it the left ear? One side meant, "Come to me, beloved," the other meant, "Sorry, my wife won't let me," but he couldn't remember which was which.

That came from his having been driving on the wrong side of the road all afternoon, he supposed. It wouldn't have mattered in this particular dream, anyway. He'd been more concerned about such niceties back in the pre-Helen period when he'd got more deeply involved with a biologist from Amherst that he'd meant to. Christabel, her name was.

How in Sam Hill had Christabel snuck into his dream, anyhow? Drat it, the Randy Shandy of yore was a respectably married man now. Peter wished Helen would manifest herself instead. He liked dreaming about Helen. He couldn't think of much about Helen that he didn't like, except that he was here and she was—where? In some quaint olde worlde teashop by now, scoffing up scones with Iduna, while he was being led up the forest path by an overexcited id. Why the flaming perdition didn't Tim and Dan come along and wake him up?

Maybe they'd decided he needed his rest, and left him to slumber among the beer pumps while they quaffed their restoratives. No, they wouldn't have allowed him to remain draped over the bar for some wandering professor to see and to deride. They'd have dragged him over and laid him down on one of those oaken benches so picturesquely hollowed by so many generations of bucolic buttocks.

His wisest course might therefore be to select a likely root and lie down upon it, perhaps conjuring up a few robins to cover him with leaves for added comfort. Then he could dream himself to sleep so that he could wake up on all levels of consciousness at once, and get the show back on the road.

Why couldn't he have simply dreamed himself out into that fine stand of hogweed? He could have got in a spot of preliminary investigation and saved himself some time. Peter could see no hogweed around here, wherever here might be. Too shady, no doubt. It was going to be a howling shame to cut down such noble trees as these. They'd have to go sometime, though, so the land could be cleared for farming. He hoped he'd wake up before that happened.

Peter was getting concerned about his companions. Dan Stott, to be sure, had *festina lente* engraven on his backbone, but Tim was brisk enough. Unless his mind wandered to trace elements. Cripes, if Dan had got to ruminating and Tim to pondering the subtler nuances of boron in the beet fields again, he could be stuck in this imaginary forest till the cows came home.

Assuming there were any cows to come. So far, Peter had seen no sign of life except that one gnat, which he'd swatted out of whatever existence it might have been supposed to possess. He was getting lonesome. Maybe that dream about the roomful of snickering students would have been preferable, after all. Why didn't something happen?

CHAPTER 2

His grandmother had always said it wasn't safe to wish for anything because if you did, you might get it. Shandy was kicking petulantly at a root, bemoaning like Arthur Guiterman's cam-u-el his too-distinguished onliness, when he got poked in the chest by a harp.

"What the hell?" was his natural reaction.

"Oh, sorry." Above the twanging of agitated harp strings, the apology came loud and clear. "Force of habit."

The speaker was, as perhaps Peter might have expected, a giant. A mere stripling among giants, to be sure: probably not more than seven feet in height and a paltry yard or so across the shoulders. Still, this was an impressive enough giant to dream up on one's first try. Peter Shandy would not have wanted a larger giant. He wasn't at all sure he wanted this one.

However, the giant's not uncomely countenance looked amiable enough, not to say contrite. " 'Tis this goddamn enchantment I be under," he was explaining. "I haven't got used to traveling without my lance. I mean, ye meet a wizard, it's ye customary etiquette of ye geste to ram ye old lance tip up against his tabard and make him confess what he hath been up to. Ye blasted wizards be always up to something."

He straightened the wreath of giant hogweed that had slid cockeyed on his flowing golden locks, hitched up the skirt of his white robe to scratch a thigh the size of an oak bole, and sighed. "I forget what ye protocol be for a bard in a situation like this. Ye wouldn't happen to recall, I misdoubt me?"

"Sorry," Shandy answered. "I'm a—er—stranger here, myself. Do I gather you are in fact a knight errant who's been turned by some form of necromancy into a traveling poet?"

"Urrgh," said the giant. "I hight Torchyld y Dewr. Highted,

I mean, until this morning. I wot not what I hight now. Torchyld yr Anobeithiol, perchance."

"Too bad," Shandy replied, knowing somehow that the former meant The Intrepid and the latter meant The Hopeless. "Not about the Torchyld part, I mean. Torchyld's a first-rate name. I know somebody with a name very much like it. As a matter of fact, you remind me—"

"Arrgh!" the giant interrupted. "Never mind that. Ye be supposed to tell me how ye hight. I remember that much anyway."

"So I am. Well, I—er—hight Peter Shandy. Actually I'm not a wizard. I'm a professor."

"A what?"

"A—er—teacher."

"Oh, a druid. Why saidst ye not so in ye first place? Dost ken any poetry?"

"Quite a lot, as a matter of fact. Have you heard the one about the young lady of Niger who smiled as she rode on a tiger?"

Torchyld clearly had not. Nor, as Shandy realized a few syllables too late, would he be likely to know the meaning of either Niger or tiger. The sample had been ill-chosen. But why did the giant have to cry about it? For crying, Torchyld incredibly was.

"Dash it all," snapped Shandy, "I didn't mean to hurt your feelings. Here, take my handkerchief and blow your nose, like a good chap."

It was then that he became aware he no longer possessed a handkerchief, nor a pocket to carry one in. Like the enchanted warrior blubbering before him, he was wearing a longish robe of what might in a romance be described as fairest white linen. To Peter it looked coarsely woven, badly wrinkled, and none too clean.

As for the handkerchief, Torchyld wouldn't have known that word either, and didn't appear to be interested. He merely sniffed a mighty sniffle and ignored the tears on his cheeks, this being evidently some kind of Golden Age when a man didn't have to go around acting manly if he didn't happen to feel like it.

"I weep for ye Lady Syglinde," he explained with simple dignity. "Ye being a druid and therefore possessed of un-bounded wisdom, I perceive a kindly spirit hath set me in thy way, that I may unto thee my woeful tale unfold. Prithee haul up a root and ease thy feet. This may take a while."

"I'm in no hurry," said Peter, draping his laundry more snugly about him and settling into the shade of a giant oak. Tim and Dan must be just about getting to work on their second pints by now, so he might as well nap a while longer. This dream was beginning to liven up.

"Okay, shoot. That is—er—unfold thy tale. What happened to Lady Syglinde? Did she get enchanted, too?"

"My Syglinde be herself an enchantment," Torchyld groaned. "Forsooth, had it not been for that old hag Dwydd, we should e'en now be wending our way to the battlements, thereon to plight our troth. Syglinde and I spend quite a lot of time plighting our troth," he admitted with what might in a less awesome figure have been described as a boyish grin. "At least we did, until Ffyffnyr disappeared."

"You did say Ffyffnyr?"

"In sooth," Torchyld replied in some surprise. "So did ye also. Why not? That be his hight."

"Yes, but who is he?"

"Meseemed ye druids be supposed to wot this stuff. He be my great-uncle Sfyn's pet griffin."

"Drat it, you can't expect me to remember the name of every griffin that comes flapping along," said Peter testily. "We dru-ids have far weightier matters to occupy our minds. What's so special about Ffyffnyr?"

"He be not a bad old scout, as griffins go. Great-uncle Sfyn hath him trained to roll over and play enchanted, sit up and beg for boiled eels, give ye his talon, all kinds of cute tricks. And when ye throne room groweth too cold, Ffyff can always breathe fire and warm ye place up."

"M'yes, I see. A comforting sort of beast to have around, no doubt. You spoke of a throne room. Your great-uncle would then be King Sfyn?"

"Aye, so he be. And I be his great-nephew and Syglinde his ward. She and I had it all fixed up we were going to get wedlocked and build ourselves a cozy little castle with our own portcullis, and settle down to raising eels in ye moat and *digrifwch* in ye royal chamber."

Shandy didn't have much trouble figuring out *digrifwch*, either. "Your own castle, eh? Then you're not in line to inherit your great-uncle's kingdom?"

"Nay, druid, I be only—let's see." Torchyld tried counting on his fingers, but gave it up as a bad job after two. "To begin with, there be his sons, Prince Edmyr, Prince Edwy, and Prince Edbert. My father was King Sfyn's nephew Lord Edolph, but *taddi* got eaten by a garefowl one day when he was out hunting sea monsters. Or perchance it was ye other way around. My mother was never clear as to ye details. She wasted away."

"I'm sorry to hear it."

"Gramercy, druid, Where was I? Oh yes. After my uncles there be Uncle Edmyr's son Dagobert. He be ye crown prince now. His brother Dilwyn used to be, but Dilwyn perished at ye last new moon of a surfeit and bloody flux. Then there be Edwy's son Owain, and Edbert's sons Gelert and Gaheris. Those be all my cousins. Ye legitimate ones, anyway. The rest count not. There be female cousins, too, but they also count not in terms of ye succession. My aunts be always nagging me to marry one of ye girls now that I be rich and famous."

"Are you, forsooth?"

"Forsooth, verily. Wist ye not? I be he that slew ye wyvern. See ye, this wyvern gan laying waste ye countryside, kidnapping fair maidens and whatnot. Eftsoons ye wyvern gan carrying off sheep, too. So then something had to be done. So I did. So I made claim to ye wyvern's hoard."

Shandy had been under the impression it was dragons that had hoards, but perhaps a wyvern counted as a kind of dragon. He thought he would not raise the question. No doubt druids were supposed to know all about wyverns, too.

"Ah, yes," he said briskly. "Speaking of wyverns, let's get back to Ffyffnyr."

"Ffyffnyr be a griffin."

"So you've already informed me. The difference being that a wyvern has only two front legs, the hinder part of its body being serpentine in form. A griffin is just an ordinary, run-of-the-mill quadrupedal cross between a lion and an eagle. With wings, needless to say. Both are members of the genus *Bestialis mythicus.*"

"I wot not of learned tongues," Torchyld answered rather sulkily. "Hast ever slain a wyvern with a disenchanted sword and two stale biscuits, druid?"

"No, I can't say I have," Shandy admitted. "Nor should I care to try. That must have been a feat unparalleled for valor, not to mention agility and resourcefulness. You used the biscuits as bait, I assume?"

"Nay," quoth Torchyld. "I but stood waiting till he got close and opened his jaws to devour me. Then I chucked ye biscuits down his gullet and rammed them into his windpipe with ye point of my sword. So when he tried to breathe fire at me, he backfired and fried his own gizzard."

"Good Lord!"

"Well may ye say so," Torchyld replied with a self-satisfied smirk. "Ye accursed sword was otherwise useless. I had essayed to hew him in twain with one blow as is my wont, but ye damned blade wouldn't even cut through ye first layer of scales. Baleful Dwydd had cast an evil spell on it and had not e'en shown ye courtesy to taunt me with her perfidy as I was setting off on my geste. She but handed me ye biscuits with a fiendish leer, and went flapping off to her turret."

"This—er—Dwydd lives right in King Sfyn's castle?"

"Aye, verily. Ye can't have a castle without a wicked hag roosting in one turret or another, ecod. It be not ye done thing. Syglinde and I had been wondering where we could find one for our own love nest. 'Tis a job to tax a wizard, tracking down a really rotten beldame these days, I tell ye. Most hags be but mean-tempered because the damp getteth into their aged bones and they lack a pet griffin to keep them warm. Syggie said perchance we might take in some poor soul who needeth a home and make believe she be evil. What difference? All this keeping up with ye Penjoneses can be carried too far, meseems."

"My sentiments exactly," Shandy told him. "Perhaps you and Lady Syglinde can start a fashion for keeping a good hag instead of a bad one."

"And why think ye I shall ever get a chance to start anything?" Torchyld snarled. "Gin I fail to get Ffyffnyr back, I be forever banished from the kingdom and Great-uncle Sfyn will marry off my darling Syglinde to yon scurvy, stinking, caitiff louse Owain."

"Your cousin Owain is also interested in your—er—much-betrothed?"

"She dealt him perforce a lusty buffet with a trencherful of boiled eels but four e'ens agone. Great-uncle Sfyn nigh brast a gut laughing."

"Then what are you blethering about? Lady Syglinde is obviously a young woman who knows how to handle herself in a clinch. And if the king is so partial to Owain, why would he have laughed?"

"It was funny," Torchyld replied. "I laughed, also. Then I wrapped a brace of eels around Owain's neck and stuffed their tails down his ugly throat and made him eat them or choke. He broke out in spots next morning. Boiled eels always give Owain spots. Great-uncle Sfyn was still laughing about ye spots, until he found out Ffyffnyr was agone."

"How did Ffyffnyr go?"

"How should I know, prithee? He went. One minute he was there trying to sneak a boiled eel off the banqueting board. The next minute he was gone. Poof."

"You observed this poof? That is to say, you actually saw the griffin disappear?"

"How could I? Have I eyes to see what was and is suddenly not? Anyway, I was up on ye battlements at ye time."

"Getting in a spot of troth-plighting while you were fresh and rested, eh?"

"Nay, I was on guard duty. A castle's safety rests on its

sentries' eyeballs. We keep aye a sharp lookout for ogres and dragons and marauding armies and suchlike."

"See many of them around these parts?"

"Off and on. Ye know how it be. Anyway, I was up there keen-eyed and vigilant, setting an example to ye lower ranks according to court protocol and military discipline. Had Ffyffnyr flown off, I could not but have seen him. I saw not, so he hath not."

"Was he in the habit of flying off?"

"Nay, Ffyffnyr might take a little spin around ye turrets when he felt ye urge, like any normal griffin, but he cameth always back. Ffyffnyr be no grifflet, ye ken, and he hath been a pet all his life. Great-uncle Sfyn's own father, Sfynwair ye Compassionate, found him in a cave barely out of ye egg, and brought him back to ye castle for Sfyn to play with. They were babes together, and they've grown old together."

Torchyld began to cry again. "Curses, it rotteth mine guts to think of yon fat old griffin in some ogre's stewpot, and Great-uncle Sfyn back there alone in ye banqueting hall with his mustache dragging in his metheglin. He be like to pine away without Ffyff, dammit."

"You don't suppose that's what somebody had in mind?" Shandy ventured.

"Ungh?"

"I don't want to raise unjust suspicions, Sir Torchyld, but might not one of your uncles, to raise a hypothetical question, have a hankering to become king in his father's stead? After all, if Prince Edmyr, Prince Edwy, and Prince Edbert all have grown sons of their own, as you told me, they can't be getting any younger themselves. The longer King Sfyn hangs on, the more likely it appears that certain of his heirs could die without ever getting a whack at the throne, doesn't it?"

"Mine uncles be not magicians," Torchyld protested. "They be but princes. In sooth, they get fed up now and then. I gainsay ye not that it be possible one of them might wish to hurry Great-uncle Sfyn along a trifle gin he foundeth a chance, but look at ye facts. A mere prince wotteth not to make a griffin go poof. A prince can't do much of anything except ride off on gestes and rescue beautiful princesses from monsters and evil wizards. My uncles have all been down that road long ago. Bethink ye, once a prince hath rescued one beautiful princess, that first princess be like to wax exceeding wroth gin he goeth off and rescueth another. I know because Uncle Edwy tried it. Aunt Edelgysa found out and beaned him with ye thighbone of a sheep."

"Gad," said Shandy. "I hadn't realized food could be such a dangerous weapon."

"Did I not tell ye about me and ye biscuits?"

"You did. Now tell me more about Ffyffnyr. Has he any distinguishing features? That is to say," Shandy amplified since Torchyld looked puzzled at his choice of words, "is he in any way different from other griffins? Aside from being old and fat, that is?"

"He weareth a collar of purest gold, richly engraven and set about with blazing gems."

"Excellent. Anything else?"

"He be red."

"Redder than most griffins, you mean?"

"Redder than any griffin other than he. I wot not what color ye griffins be whence ye cometh, druid, but around here they be mostly brownish yellow with green and purple streaks. Sometimes find we a griffin that be all green or all purple or kind of plaid, but no man ne yet no maid hath ever before nor since found a red one. That be why Sfynwair ye Compassionate kept Ffyff in ye first place. Ffyff waxeth somewhat gray around ye muzzle now, but still gleameth he as red as ye lips of my beauteous Syglinde."

"You're not going to cry any more, I hope," Shandy pleaded. "Try to keep your mind on the griffin. When did you find out he was gone?"

"When ye guards came to seize me."

"They seized you? Off the battlements, you mean?"

"Nay, druid, I said not they seized me. I said they came to. I tied them together in pairs by ye hairs of ye heads, and dangled them over ye parapet until they changed their minds and let me walk down by myself. So I went into ye great hall and found

Great-uncle Sfyn waxing wrother than ever I have seen him wax before. All my aunts and uncles were standing around giving me dirty looks, and Dwydd was hopping and cackling and pointing her finger at me, in accordance with standard court procedure for evil hags. Dwydd wotteth her job, I'll say that for her. So then everybody started hueing and crying about what had I done with Ffyffnyr. Then I realized Syglinde wasn't there."

"Because nobody was getting beaned with a trencher, I suppose?"

"In sooth. So I gan yelling what ye hell were they all yelling about and what had they done with Syglinde? So Uncle Edmyr said never mind Syglinde, where was Ffyffnyr? So I asked him how was I supposed to wot?"

"A reasonable question."

"So then Dwydd hopped and cackled some more, and ye gist of her cackling was that I had spirited Ffyffnyr away by ye same mystical power I used to kill ye wyvern. That be a lot of dragon feathers and I told them so. But they believed me not."

"Why, do you suppose?"

"Because Uncle Edmyr and Uncle Edwy and ye rest be ashamed for that they themselves fared not forth to slay ye wyvern, and ye women are ashamed of their men for being a bunch of *llwfryns* but dare not say so. Gin they can all fool themselves into believing I, a mere great-nephew of the king, performed that mighty deed of valor by a cantrip spell instead of with a disenchanted sword and—"

"Two stale biscuits," said Shandy. "A shrewd observation, Sir Torchyld. So that's their story and you're stuck with it."

"True, O druid. Great-uncle Sfyn commanded me to search ye world over if need be, until I find Ffyffnyr, or ne'er again will I embrace my darling Syglinde. And just as I was leaving, Dwydd slapped this goddamn enchantment on me to make my search impossible. So here I be with no sword, no lance, no horse, nothing but a harp and a tin ear, forsooth. What the *uffern* be I to do?"

"What would you do if you were a real bard?"

"Oh, meseems I would charm ye birds of ye air and ye beasts

of ye field and ye minds and hearts of men and women with ye power of my voice and all that *ffolineb*. How do I wot what I would do? I have ne'er been a bard before, and I be not one now. And I be doomed ne'er to betroth my Syglinde again!"

"Drat it," snapped Peter, "if you don't quit blubbering, I'll disenchant you myself."

"Canst, druid?" Torchyld grabbed his arm in a grip like a griffin's. "Why said ye not so in ye first place?"

"M'well, frankly, I didn't mean that in quite the way it came out. That is to say, we druids have to—er—observe the druidical protocol, you know. We can't simply go around disenchanting people without—er—studying their cases first, you know."

"Nay, I wot not," howled the ill-made bard. "I but wot gin ye fail to disenchant me and help me get Syglinde back, I wot to wrap thy neck around thy knees and use ye for a football."

CHAPTER 3

An anthropologist might have been interested to learn King Sfyn's great-nephew played football. Peter Shandy was only concerned with whether his oversized new acquaintance really meant what he said. This dream was getting awfully physical.

"Then let's—er—get on with it," he said. "The first thing—"

"Ye first thing be to get rid of this accursed harp," Torchyld interrupted, giving the instrument a contemptuous twang.

"Not on your life. One never knows when one may need a harp."

"What for?"

Peter couldn't think what for, so he put on what he hoped was a profound and druidical expression. Torchyld did have the grace to look somewhat abashed, though he gave the harp another jangle, evoking horrible discords and causing some hitherto silent rooks to begin squawking pettishly in the tree-tops.

"There, goddamit," came a voice from somewhere. "I told you we were dead. I hear heavenly harps, and angels singing."

"A malignant shade," cried Torchyld. "Aroint! Aroint!"

"Aroint, hell," bellowed Shandy. "Tim! Hey, Tim! Over this way."

"Pete! Cripes, are you dead, too?"

Timothy Ames could still put on a fair burst of speed for a short sprint. He came bounding down the forest path, followed at a more stately pace by Daniel Stott and his cheese. Both, like Peter, were wearing what looked like bedraggled nightgowns. Both had white coverings over their heads, secured by golden bands around their foreheads. Tim was carrying a ceremonial golden sickle that made him look like Father

Time. He caught sight of Peter, glanced back at Dan and down at his own garb, and snorted.

"Damn, I thought this was the pearly gates, but it looks more like an Arab oilmen's convention. Where in hell are we? Or should I rephrase the question?"

"Your guess is as good as mine," Peter told him. "All I can tell you is that you appear to have butted into a dream I was having. Happy to have you aboard, of course. Meet Sir Torchyld, an enchanted warrior."

"The devil he is. Who enchanted him?"

Tim moved closer to the giant and squinted upward. He was without his spectacles and hearing aid, no doubt because they would have been out of period with the golden sickle and other accoutrements, but he was managing better than might have been expected.

"God, Pete," he said after he'd completed his examination, "doesn't he remind you of the President?"

For the three wayfarers there was only one President: namely, Thorkjeld Svenson, head thunderbolt hurler at Balaclava Agricultural College. Peter nodded.

"He's younger and more talkative, and he cries a lot—though I'll admit he has plenty to cry about," Peter added when the giant began to look truculent, "but I'll admit the resemblance is pretty frightening. Perhaps, Tim, you'd like to tell him the first name of his fair lady."

"Cripes, doesn't he know?"

"Certainly he knows. I just thought he'd appreciate a demonstration of your—er—druidical wisdom."

"Is that what we're supposed to be? Okay, son, your girl friend's name is Sieglinde and she's going to bean you with that harp if she finds you out here running around in your nightshirt. What's this dream of yours all about anyway, Pete?"

"I'm not sure yet. Hi, Dan, join the party."

Daniel Stott hove up to the group, parked his cheese on a convenient oak bole, and regarded them with a steady, benevolent gaze.

"Peter, old friend, well met. And this would be an ancestor, or what might perhaps be deemed a prototype, of our esteemed President, in the somewhat surprising and one would have thought inappropriate guise of a Welsh bard."

"I be under enchantment," Torchyld informed him.

"Ah, that would explain the incongruity."

"What I don't understand," said Timothy Ames, "is what he's doing in Wales. The President's a Swede, at least his ancestors were."

"They were Vikings, I believe. Norsemen found the British Isles an ideal target for their acts of pillage and rapine, and no doubt intermarried freely with the natives. Or not, as the case might have been. According to accepted theories of reincarnation, it is possible for the entity to manifest in diverse locations and situations over a wide time span. The druids believed in transmigration, you know, although perhaps possibly not in reincarnation as we regard it."

"Who regards it?" barked Timothy Ames. "Go ahead, Dan, tell him his sweetheart's name."

"I gather you expect me to say Sieglinde. She would be a lady of noblest mien and remarkable force of character, perhaps a trifle slender in form for my personal taste but extraordinarily personable withal. Would this gentleman, whom I deem to hight Thorkjeld or a reasonable facsimile thereof, care for further information about his lady?"

"Yes," howled Torchyld, bursting into tears again, "where be she?"

Shandy took it upon himself to explain. "Sir Torchyld's having a spot of bother with his great-uncle Sfyn."

"Dying Jesus," Tim groaned. "Not that old goat who seduced Hilda Horsefall over at Lumpkin Corners? I thought he was back in Sweden."

"Drat it, Tim, whose dream is this, anyway? Let me explain, can't you? The thing is that King Sfyn, as he happens to be at the moment, whenever the moment may be, has lost his pet griffin. Sir Torchyld is accused of having spirited it away. Therefore, King Sfyn has in turn hidden Lady Syglinde somewhere and says Torchyld can't have her back until he produces the griffin in reasonable condition."

"Why in only reasonable condition?" asked Dan Stott. "Does this griffin have a medical problem?"

"He's old, that's all, and a bit on the hefty side. He's spry enough otherwise. Isn't that right, Sir Torchyld?"

The giant wiped his nose on the back of his hand. "How can I say? Ffyff could be—"

"Come, come," said Peter briskly. "Grown-up giants don't cry. When did you last see Ffyffnyr? That's the griffin's name," he explained in an aside to Ames and Stott.

"Gin they ken Syglinde's name, how come they kenned not Ffyff's?" Torchyld demanded.

"Our particular branch of the druids happens to specialize in women rather than griffins, that's all. Please answer the question. Did you see the creature this morning?"

"Nay. I went perforce on duty at cockcrow. Ffyff never ariseth so early gin he can help it."

"Where does he sleep?"

"Across Great-uncle Sfyn's threshold, in sooth."

"H'm, a well-trained griffin. But you told me Ffyffnyr was in the act of stealing boiled eels off the breakfast table this morning when he disappeared. How did you know that?"

"Well, he always doth."

"Why eels?" Dan Stott wanted to know.

"They slither down easily. Ffyff has but few fangs left."

"Have you tried him on—"

"Later, Dan," said Peter. "Then, Sir Torchyld, you don't actually know whether the griffin did in fact disappear from the banqueting hall."

"They all said he did."

"Who all?"

"Aunt Aldora, Aunt Edelgysa, Aunt Gwynedd, Uncle Edmyr, Uncle Edwy, Uncle Edbert, Cousin Dagobert, Cousin Owain, Cousin Gelert, Cousin Gaheris, Cousin Gwendolyn, Cousin Guinevere, Cousin—"

"Thank you. Precisely how did they say the griffin disappeared?"

"I told ye, he but went. Poof."

"He didn't—er—take wing?"

"Meaneth ye did he fly away? Methinks one so learned might try to talk straight. Nay, he took not wing. Some of them would have said so gin he had flown, would they not? Anyway, Ffyff's right wing hath bothered him these past few days. Syglinde hath been rubbing it with warm eel grease."

Stott raised his eyebrows, slowly so as not to tax the facial muscles. "Eel grease? I should rather have thought a decoction of—"

"Right, Dan," said Peter. "Sir Torchyld, can you tell me precisely what your uncles and your cousins and your aunts said with regard to the griffin's disappearance?"

"How many times will ye ask, druid? They said he was there and then he was not. Poof."

"Did they go looking for him?"

"Aye, they looked. Great-uncle Sfyn drove them to ye hunt like partridges before ye beaters. They hunted high, they hunted low, e'en in places too small for Ffyff to fit into."

"How big is he?"

"Ordinary griffin size. Gin he standeth on his hind claws, he can just about rest his front ones on my shoulders. He cometh thus to me when he craveth his chin whiskers to be scratched."

"I am reminded of our prize boar, Balthazar of Balaclava," said Daniel Stott. "There is a certain poignancy about the endearing little ways of very large beasts."

"No doubt," said Peter. "Well, boys, it looks to me as if we're not going to get anywhere with this case of the gone griffin unless we hightail it straight to King Sfyn's castle and hear some firsthand accounts of Ffyffnyr's disappearance for ourselves. Dan, you and Sir Torchyld can compare notes about Ffyffnyr and Balthazar on the way," he added kindly.

"What way?" snarled their difficult new acquaintance. "Think ye we should ever get back to ye castle, druid? Dwydd hath by now barred ye path by many a fell enchantment."

"Who's Dwydd?" Tim wanted to know.

"King Sfyn's resident hag," Peter told him.

"Oh, he's got one, too, has he?" Tim knew all about resident hags. "Then what's the big mystery? I'd be willing to bet my shirt, if I knew where the hell I left it, that griffin's around the castle somewhere. Stuck up over a downspout disguised as a gargoyle, most likely. How the hell did we get into this, Pete?"

"Don't ask me, Tim. All I know is, when you and Dan went into the men's room of that pub, I walked on ahead into the bar. There wasn't a soul around, not even the bartender. I was standing there working up a thirst and thinking how shiny the pump handles were when, as Sir Torchyld here would say, poof. Here I was and there he came. That's my story. What's yours?"

"Same thing, just about. When Dan and I went into the bar, you weren't there. We thought you must have stepped out to take a gander at that hogweed down in the meadow, so we were going to go ahead and order our drinks. But the bartender wasn't there, either. We coughed and flapped around, you know how you do, thinking somebody would hear us and come out, but nobody did. So then I said to Dan, why didn't we go ahead and draw one for ourselves? If the guy never showed up, we could just leave the money. So we both went behind the bar. Dan was getting us a couple of glasses and I was trying to figure out which pump was for the bitter when we poofed, too."

"Your hypothesis, Peter," said Daniel Stott, "is that we are sharing a dream. May I venture an alternative suggestion? I believe we are jointly experiencing something quite other than a mere sleep-induced vagary."

"Such as what?"

"Simply a situation of a type that appears to be relatively frequent in this part of the world. As you know, I have been bountifully blessed with offspring. When my children were small, we maintained the homely old custom of reading aloud. Knowing this, my sister Matilda kept us well supplied with what she deemed to be suitable reading matter. Matilda's penchant was for British authors who wrote about children falling down rabbit holes or stepping into wardrobes and finding themselves thenceforth involved with adventures of a nature which at the time seemed to me fantastical. I therefore assumed these to be works of fiction. Now I realize they must have been mere vignettes of local history. That public house evidently functions in a manner somewhat akin to a wardrobe or a rabbit hole. We may perhaps consider ourselves fortunate to have encountered Sir Torchyld instead of a well-dressed rabbit or a talking lion."

"I'd have settled for a rabbit," said Tim.

"I'd have settled for a pint," sighed Peter. "Drat it, why didn't we pick another pub?"

"Because you wanted to stop there and look at the goddamn hogweed, that's why," his old comrade snarled back.

"Friends," Dan interposed, "let us strive to avoid dissension. Dimmed by the passage of time though my recollection of Matilda's tales must inevitably be, it strikes me that any show of disunity was always prejudicial to the outcome of any escapade in which the protagonists found themselves caught up."

"M'yes," said Peter. "I'm afraid you may be right, Dan. All right. We're down the rabbit hole and I'm the one to blame."

"Indeed, Peter, accepting full responsibility is not your privilege. I say this in no contentious spirit, but as a simple fact. We are equally grown men, and men of reason. Our right of choice is as valid as yours. Had we urged you to drive on, you would no doubt have acceded to our wishes. We chose instead to stop with you. Therefore, we must insist on our right to share the blame, if blame there be, for our present plight."

"Gad, Dan," said Peter, deeply touched, "I had no idea you were a man of so profound a philosophical bent."

"Anyone who communes much with hogs inevitably becomes a philosopher. Would you care for some cheese?"

"I would," said Torchyld. "My fast hath not been broke since yester e'en. I meant to eat after my watch was over, but I got no chance, with everybody yammering at me and Greatuncle Sfyn banishing me and Dwydd enchanting me and my darling Syglinde—"

"Give him some cheese, quick," said Peter.

"By all means," Stott replied. "Tim, might I trouble you for the loan of that golden sickle? Though a sickle is not, I fear, the ideal instrument for cutting cheese."

"Ye could hack it with my disenchanted sword," Torchyld

offered. "Ye blade be no good for anything else. I doubt not
that be why Dwydd let me keep it."

He hauled the mangled blade from underneath his robe and
whacked a mighty hunk off the cheese. As he started to munch,
Peter Shandy reached for the sword.

"Let's see that thing for a minute, if you don't mind. Tim,
what do you think?"

The elderly gnome brought the blade close to his eyes, then
ran a thorny thumb along its edge. "I'd say some bastard's
disenchanted this sword by whanging it against a rock. You
want it reenchanted, son, or prince, or whatever we're supposed to call you?"

"Gin ye wottest to work so great a charm, archdruid,"
Torchyld replied with his mouth full of cheese, "ye may call me
anything ye crave to."

"Just let me find something to use for a whetstone. Ought to
be a halfway decent stone kicking around here. Ah, just the
ticket."

Among the arcane skills Timothy Ames had learned as a boy
on a farm was how to put an edge on a tool with a hand-held
stone and a judicious application of elbow grease. While
Torchyld wolfed cheese and gazed in wonderment, Tim
stroked at the nicked and battered blade. When Tim gave out,
Peter took over. By the time the two disenchanters were telling
each other they guessed maybe now she'd do, Torchyld was
wiping his mouth on his forearm and Dan Stott was regarding
the remains of his cheese with grave concern.

"Ye be great wizards," cried the young giant. "Now prithee
disenchant me."

"I expect you'll be disenchanted enough before this expedition's over," Peter told him. "Which way is King Sfyn's castle?
Ready, gentlemen? Let's go."

"Where to?" asked Timothy Ames.

Well might he ask. Directly in front of them, blocking their
way, stood a solid mass of giant hogweed.

CHAPTER 4

"I told ye so," said Torchyld. "She will not let us gae."

"She?" said Tim. "You don't mean the resident hag?"

"None other. She groweth yon evil weed by a foul enchantment. Ye path was clear when I came over it but a small while
hence."

"You sure it was the same path, son?"

"How many paths dost think we have, forsooth? Verily, archdruid, wert ye not so aged and venerable, I'd call that a
damned silly question. What kingdom be so proud and foolish
as to have more than one path in a given direction?"

Tim snorted. Shandy sighed, thinking of the four-lane high-
ways they'd traveled to get to that ill-omened pub.

"You've been walking along this path, then, ever since you
left the castle?" he asked.

"Where else would a bard walk?"

"You didn't go foraging in the woods along the way, to see if
you could find your great-uncle's griffin?"

"To what end? I wot Dwydd hath him enchanted, same as
me. Mine eyes avail not to see him until she or ye break ye
enchantment. Nay, I but slouched along twanging this asinine
harp. I was trying to think up a rhyme for Syglinde, gin ye care
to ken. I thought perchance I could charm her to me with my
bardry, but I be hopeless at rhymes. Everything be hopeless.
Nevermore shall I—Look out!"

"Cripes," gasped Tim. "The damned stuff's chasing us."

Even as they watched in horror, the hogweed plants were
sending up shoots like pikestaffs, crowding forward to envelop
them.

"Ah, yes," said Daniel Stott, securing the remnant of his
cheese and taking a giant step backward. "My sons and I ob-

served a similar phenomenon on a television broadcast some years ago. In that instance the plants were destroyed by having seawater pumped on them. However, those were of a different species called, I believe, trifids. I question whether seawater would prove efficacious against *Heracleum mantegazzianum.*"

"I question where we'd be able to lay our hands on a pump around here, not to mention a sea," said Peter. "This is the damnedest thing I've ever seen. That hogweed's growing faster than corn in Iowa. We'd better get off this path. Torchyld, where can we go?"

His question was rhetorical. There was only one way open to them and they took it, around the bole of the biggest oak and on through the forest. For a while they seemed to be getting ahead of the hogweed. Then all of a sudden, it was surrounding them, crowding them up against a wall of rock.

"Quick," shouted Torchyld. "Here be a cave."

Fighting off the bristly, venomous leaves, they followed his lead inside. At once, the plants grew solidly across the cave's mouth, blocking any chance of egress.

"It almost looks as if the hogweed meant to pin us up in here," Shandy panted. "I wonder why."

"If we are imprisoned without food or water for any length of time," Stott began lugubriously, then caught himself. "At least we still have a modicum of cheese," he finished in a more hopeful tone, for the Stotts were men of valor.

"Well, we can't stay here watching the goddamn hogweed grow," Tim fretted. "I vote we hunt for another way out."

"Have we reason to hope there might in fact be another exit?" Dan inquired.

"I shouldn't be surprised if there are several," Peter answered, trying to sound hearty. "The rock formations are mostly limestone around here. Limestone's highly water-soluble, as you know, and this is a rainy climate. The cave roof may have broken through in any number of places. I'd only suggest we try to leave a trail of some sort, so that we can find our way back to this opening if we have to. The cave may go on for a considerable distance."

And wind up at a dead end, for all his brave talk. He didn't have to tell them that.

"How can we leave a trail?" Torchyld asked him.

"Good question," Peter admitted. "Tom Sawyer did it with smudges of candle black, which brings up another interesting question. How are we going to see our way? It's already dark enough here by the entrance, with those infernal hogweed plants blocking out the daylight. I don't suppose anybody thought to bring matches?"

Even as he asked, Peter knew the question was ridiculous. All he personally had in his possession at the moment were this dratted bedsheet around his body and the buskins on his feet. Except for Torchyld's harp and what was left of Dan's cheese, the others were in no better case, barring their meager arsenal of the freshly reenchanted sword and a golden sickle that wouldn't cut anything except, presumably, mistletoe. It wasn't much to equip a spelunking expedition with.

"I might have a lightning bug or two on me," Tim remarked. "I think I've picked up a fair assortment of vermin."

"I will guide you."

The voice was soft and mushy-sounding, and came from somewhere down around Peter's knees. He looked down but could see nothing. Then, somehow, the sound began to glow.

"Who—what are you?" he stammered.

"I be your guide. Ye must follow me. There be no other way. See, e'en now ye weeds grow thicker."

That, they were appalled to realize, was true. Now no gleam of light whatever could be seen from the cave's mouth. The hogweed had formed an impenetrable wall. The glow slithered over toward the opening, allowing them a sickening glimpse of hairy, turgid green stems bulging inward, either from the weight of other stems pressing against them or because they were trying to root themselves in the solid rock floor of the cave.

"Come," urged the voice. "Ye have no time to lose."

"But ye trail," cried Torchyld.

"It would be useless. Ye can ne'er come back. Ye hogweed will not let ye."

"But you do know of a way out?" Peter entreated.

"I know all ye ways. Come, they grow impatient."

The mass of hogweed was producing an eerie sound now. It must have been caused by the pressure of stems and leaves rubbing together, but it sounded horribly like the squealing roar of an infuriated wild boar, hell-bent on annihilating whatever came in his way.

"My friends," said Dan Stott, "I know that sound. It is of the sort to send the stoutest heart scrambling over the side of the pigpen. The fortuitous appearance of some mysterious guide is not without precedent in the literature to which I earlier alluded. Be this apparition benign or malevolent, the accepted procedure is to accept its proffered assistance. And indeed," he added as the grunts grew in volume and bits of limestone began to crumble away from around the mouth of the cave, "we have no other choice. After you, my stalwart companions."

"Oh, all right," grumbled Tim, "if you say so. I just wish to Christ I knew how we wound up having to follow a goddamn lit-up talking caterpillar through the middle of nowhere."

Whatever the creature might be, if it was a creature at all, it seemed to know its stuff. It wriggled along the cave floor emitting just enough light for the party to see where to put their feet. Its glow didn't penetrate to the upper reaches of the cave, but they knew the ceiling must be high because Torchyld had not yet complained of a bumped head.

None of them said much of anything, in fact, until Peter remarked, "At least we needn't worry about water to drink."

The floor and walls were damp, even puddly in spots. The voice explained courteously that the wetness was due to condensation, and that it was the water dripping down and dissolving minerals from the rock that produced the odd formations they encountered on the cave floor. Much more interesting ones hung from the ceiling, it said. The glow regretted it was not powerful enough to illuminate these latter for their edification.

Shandy, with equal courtesy, told the glow that the hanging ones were properly called stalactites and the sticking-up ones stalagmites. The glow replied that was most interesting and thanked him for the information. One got few opportunities for learned discourse in the cave, it said.

"Do you get much—er—traffic here?" Shandy asked.

"A fair amount. Animals, mostly. Dull creatures, by and large. And ye occasional strayed peasant or beleaguered warrior."

"Any damsels in distress?" Torchyld asked guilefully, thinking no doubt of his vanished Syglinde.

"We have been very slow in ye damsel department," sighed the voice. "I really cannot recall how long it's been since a weeping maiden happened along. One tends to lose track of ye passage of time down here, ye ken. But one mustn't complain. It be a living. Pray watch ye feet here, we be coming to a rather sticky bit. Perhaps two of ye might care to wait here until I light ye other two across?"

"I think we'd rather stick together," said Shandy.

He was feeling more and more uneasy, and sensed his companions were, too. Affable though it might be, a disembodied glow was hardly the most reassuring of couriers.

Peter would have liked to ask the glow something about itself, but he was finding he needed his breath for more immediate purposes. The walking, which hadn't been any too smooth at best, was now abominable. "Rather sticky" had been merely an early example of the British penchant for understatement, he supposed. Could this be an English rather than a Welsh glow? Surely they hadn't walked far enough to be back across the border.

This was no time for speculation. The roof had got low enough that they had to move at a sort of running squat. Between ducking stalactites and tripping over ill-placed stalagmites, slipping on wet patches and sliding down sudden inclines, Peter had all he could do to save his bones.

The glow wasn't being a great deal of help here. It kept chittering remarks like, "Prithee exercise caution," and "Mind ye stalagmite," but its luminescence didn't seem to be working as well as it had earlier, and it always happened to be off around a corner just when the need to see where one was stepping became most urgent.

Perhaps it was rather a dull glow, after all. Or perhaps it didn't function well under such adverse conditions as these. Or perhaps—Peter preferred not to think of any more perhapses.

Once when he slipped, he came nose-to-puddle with a sort of natural drinking fountain in the rock, where drips were falling into a bowl-like depression and staying there. Being thirsty, he essayed an experimental lick. The water tasted like ground-up chalk, a flavor neither surprising in the circumstances nor displeasing to one who'd spent so much of his life in front of a blackboard. Peter slurped a satisfying mouthful and found himself not only refreshed but also, if he wasn't being fanciful, a trifle better able to see his way around the cave.

He'd have invited his companions to take a drink, too, but the glow had somehow recharged its batteries and was putting on a burst of light and speed. The rest were hurrying to keep up with it, and Peter knew he must do the same. He still couldn't see well enough to find his way by himself, and he could vaguely make out at least three separate tunnels branching off up ahead. God forbid he should take the wrong one and get separated from his group. They were in deep enough trouble already.

CHAPTER 5

Or were they? Could this dream turned into a nightmare be winding down? A quick turn in the tunnel chosen by the glow was bringing them out, not into the forest, but to a cottage built right up against the mouth of the cave.

The cottage was definitely on the primitive side, but what did they care? Log benches, a rude trestle table set with one wooden trencher and a few wooden spoons, a fire of faggots burning on the puncheon floor and sending a reasonable percentage of its smoke up through a hole in the peak of the roof were paradise enow. A rude pot was set on stones over the fire, and a woman was stirring the pot. It would have been impossible to say how old she might be. Probably forty and looked a hundred, Shandy thought cynically. At any rate, when she heard them coming, she looked up from her cooking and greeted them pleasantly enough.

"Good e'en to ye, wayfarers. Ye have come a fearsome journey, I doubt not. Sit ye down and rest ye."

"Right gladly," said Torchyld. Being the youngest and spryest, he immediately pinched the best seat on the benches. "What manner of woman be ye, to dwell in so parlous a place?"

"It be none so parlous once ye get used to it," she replied. "Ye cave be handy for storing my food in the winter."

"By Cerridwen, then ye must be a hearty eater."

"Did you say Cerridwen?" Even as he was easing off his left buskin, for his feet had taken some hard knocks during their long stumble through the cave, Daniel Stott perked up his ears.

"I did," Torchyld replied in some surprise. "Wouldn't ye?"

"I might."

Dan stood up. Even with one bare foot and a graze on his bald head sustained by sudden contact with the cave ceiling during that last arduous scramble, he appeared majestic and almost frightening through the haze of woodsmoke from the ill-vented fire.

"Who's Cerridwen?" asked Tim, trying to act nonchalant in the face of his colleague's sudden awesomeness.

"Cerridwen," Stott drew a long breath, "was the sow goddess, Gwion's enemy in the Romance of Taliesin. Robert Graves described her as a barley goddess, equated by the learned Dr. McCulloch with the Sow Demeter, also known as Phorcis. I confess I have not thoroughly mastered the convolutions of Graves's text on the subject, for I am not a quick-thinking man. However, I have what my students would call a gut feeling that in our present circumstances it may be well for us not to take the name of Cerridwen lightly."

"I agree," said Shandy, feeling a sudden chill despite the warmth of the fire.

As an expert on grains, he'd read a few things about barley goddesses. He wished Torchyld hadn't mentioned Cerridwen, and he had a hunch the old woman did, too. She was casting uneasy glances toward the roughly tanned cowhide that served as a door to the hut.

The place was windowless, so Peter couldn't tell whether it was dark yet, but he could see no gleam of daylight through the smokehole. He couldn't see much in general. After hours of straining to follow the glow through the cave, the smoke was making his eyes sting abominably. Tim, whose vision was none too great anyway, appeared to be having a hard time. Dan Stott didn't seem to be much bothered. Either he was still in a state of elevation over the Sow Goddess, or else he hadn't yet got around to noticing his discomfort.

As for young Torchyld, he was probably used to conditions not much better than these, though no doubt a good deal flossier in the trimmings. He was sprawled on the bench with his buskins off and his feet to the fire as if he owned the place. The crone evidently found his arrogance entirely acceptable.

She merely got the trencher from the table and filled it with whatever she'd been stirring in the pot.

"Will it please you, sirs, to sup?"

"What's in that stuff?" demanded Tim, always the soul of tact.

"Naught save a gutted rabbit and a few pot herbs. None such grand fare as noblemen be wont to eat, but the best a poor widow's table can afford."

"I'm sure it's delicious," Peter said politely. In fact it didn't smell much worse than a New England boiled dinner after the cabbage goes in.

"Let him taste it first," Tim insisted, jerking his head at young Torchyld.

"It shall be as ye archdruid wishes," said the giant, picking up one of the wooden spoons and scooping a mighty dollop out of the trencher.

"Archdruid be he? Oh, I am indeed honored beyond all hooping," cried the old woman, bobbing what was perhaps the great-grandmother of a curtsy. "Let me lay down a skin for thy feet, exalted archdruid."

Tim looked apprehensive, but all she did was fetch a sheepskin from the heap of dried rushes in the corner that was no doubt her bed, and spread it under the bench where he sat. Then she took down a bundle of herbs from a peg on the wall, and strewed them over the sheepskin.

" 'Tis fleabane," she explained. " 'Twould not be seemly that ye august fleas privileged to sup on ye archdruid's venerable hide be mixt with ye common breed. I would crave to so honor you all, noble sirs; but alas, I have but one sheepskin and no more fleabane."

"That's quite all right," said Peter. "We appreciate your kind thought. How's the stew, Torchyld?"

Torchyld only nodded and scooped out some more. Taking the act as a sign of approval and realizing they'd better dig in or go hungry, the others picked up spoons, too.

Eating out of a common dish was not an agreeable change for them, but at least they each had his own spoon. Shandy realized such a refinement might not be customary in so mean a hovel. Maybe the old woman carved them to peddle as souvenirs to the travelers she succored. He wondered what else she might do for a living.

"Ye forest feedeth me," she remarked, as though she'd read his thought. "It giveth me nuts and berries, and herbs for my pot and sticks for my fire. Sometimes I have the great luck to find a rabbit in my snare. This was a fine, fat one and would have fed me for three suns to come. Be it to your liking, noble sirs?"

"Excellent," said Shandy, feeling like a worm for having taken the rabbit from a poor widow's mouth. "Aren't you having any yourself?"

"Sir, ye jest! Is it for the likes of me to break bread with ye likes of you?"

"No," said Torchyld with his mouth full. "She can scrape ye pot when we have done. What be to drink, crone?"

"But an humble brew of mine own concoction, noble sire."

"Fetch it forth." Torchyld tossed a gnawed rabbit bone over his shoulder and reached for the drinking horn. She pulled it back.

"Nay, noble bard. Ye revered archdruid should drink first."

"But I be a king's great-nephew under enchantment."

"With all respect, young sir, every third male person who cometh through my cave be a king's great-nephew under enchantment, could one believe ye tales they tell. Were I to slight ye great archdruid, I might be put under an enchantment far more grave than thine."

"Have it thine own way. I yield not to rank but to respect for gray hairs," Torchyld growled, chucking another bone on the floor and pawing around in the trencher for the last morsel of meat. "Be this all ye have, ugly hag?"

"There be but a sup of broth in the pot," she faltered. "I was hoping—"

"Bring it here."

"Stay," said Daniel Stott. "Let our gracious hostess have her share. I suggest, madam, that while you eat what remains of this palatable stew, for which we thank you heartily, I melt my piece of cheese in your cooking pot. You would not by chance have any bacon in the house?"

"I have but one small rind, your worship."

"That will suffice. The bacon, you see, is suspended over the pot so that its fat drips down and imparts its flavor to the cheese. The melted cheese can then be served over crackers or toasted bread, should any be available."

"I have flat cakes of grounden acorns," she replied. "They could be atoasting by my fire whilst melteth ye cheese. 'Tis a woundily fine substitute for a rabbit, forsooth. Never in this land hath any heard of such a dish."

"By George, Dan, I think you've just invented Welsh rabbit," cried Peter. "How's the hooch, Tim?"

"Better than Jemima used to make," said the archdruid, his eyeballs wobbling slightly.

Jemima Ames, Tim's late wife, had probably been the worst cook in the world. Her essays into winemaking had been among her more picturesque fiascos, setting the air of Balaclava Junction alive with flying corks, and rattling the toenails of anybody who dared to taste the results. "Better than Jemima's" was faint praise, but it was something. Tim took another sip to confirm his decision, then passed the horn to Stott. Dan in turn quaffed, gagged, and handed it along to Torchyld, who was looking pretty waxy by now. He took a mighty swig and gave the rest to Peter.

"Ye dregs for thee, druid, since ye begrudge a desolated lover his small meed of consolation."

"Drat it, I don't begrudge you anything. I just don't see why this poor woman has to be done out of her supper because she's had the decency to come to our rescue. Would you care for a drop of the craythur, madam?"

Without drinking any himself, Peter offered the horn to their hostess. He'd have preferred to think he did it out of politeness, but the fact was, he didn't like what he saw in the horn. Either she'd left a dead spider down at the tip, or else that strange acuity of vision he'd experienced after he'd drunk the water in the cave was still working.

The woman refused. "Nay, kind and noble druid, strong

waters be not meet for poor though pious widows. Except maybe a nip now and then to chase ye damp from mine ancient bones," she amended, slurping down the last of the rabbit broth before Torchyld could change his mind and grab it. "Drink ye and be merry. I will refill ye horn. Come, sir druid, ye knowest it be discourteous to turn down ye drinking horn while yet ye revel be hardly begun. Humble though mine entertainment be, ye wilt surely not do me the affront to refuse it."

"For Christ's sake, Pete, don't insult the poor woman," Tim hiccuped. "Go ahead, have a slug. Good for what ails you."

"If you insist."

Peter raised the horn, waited till a downdraft blew smoke in everybody's eyes, then quickly dumped the remains of the drink into the straw on the earthen floor behind him. "Thank you, madam. Most refreshing. How's the cheese coming, Dan?"

"Nicely, Peter, though in view of the lack of plates, I believe I may have invented not a Welsh rabbit but a fondue. We can best eat this, I think, by dipping pieces of the acorn cake into the pot. I will step outside and obtain some sharp twigs to serve as forks."

"Nay," cried the woman of the house. "Set ye no foot ayond this door until after cockcrow. Great though be thy magic, more terrible forces be now at work in yon forest. This hut be thine only refuge. Ye black forces dare not approach my fire. Stay and be merry. See, here be ye cake for ye dipping and here be more drink for your pleasure."

She refilled the drinking horn and handed it again to Tim. He took another swig and settled back on the bench, his beard bristling upward like a contented cat's whiskers. Again the horn passed from hand to hand. Again Peter only feigned to drink and sent it along to his clamant benchmate, Torchyld.

Dan's melted cheese was a great success. They had no trouble scooping it out of the pot, since the acorn cakes were about the heft of cedar shingles. Shandy made sure the old woman got some, and she ate it in an apparent state of ecstasy.

"To think so fine a dish could come out of my old cooking pot! Ye be indeed great men, gin men ye be."

"I already told ye I be ye great-nephew of a king," Torchyld muttered, though with some difficulty. He was already on the verge of coma, as well he might have been, considering his traumatic day and his feats with the drinking horn.

Tim was asleep even before Torchyld. Dan might or might not have been. His ruminative habit sometimes made it hard to tell. Even the widow, who'd been sneaking a nip for her bones every time she refilled the horn, must be half-seas over by now.

Peter decided he might as well go through the motions of sleeping, too. There was nothing more tedious than being the only one sober among a pack of flaked-out roisterers. When the old woman lurched into the mouth of the cave and brought out armloads of fresh rushes to cover the floor for their comfort, Peter collapsed on one of the heaps, made sure his druidical robe was decently covering his lower elevations, and mingled his snores with the rest.

But he kept his eyes half open. He was still uneasy about what he might or might not have seen at the bottom of that drinking horn.

CHAPTER 6

Maybe he'd dropped off for a minute or two. The old woman was crouched by the fire now, feeding it with little sticks. Peter couldn't imagine what kind of wood they might be. They were burning with an odd, greenish brown flame; giving off a powerful, musty odor nothing like ordinary woodsmoke. Maybe they weren't tree branches, but stalks of some herb or other. Fleabane would have been nice. Like Adam, he was sure by now he had 'em. Or else it was just prickles from the rushes he was lying on.

So this was what it had been like in the halcyon days of yore, he thought drowsily. The puncheon floor wasn't intolerable to him now, but how would it feel to aging bones on a winter's night, with the wind howling in around the edges of that cowhide door, and nothing to keep one from freezing to death but a fire of twigs and a rotten sheepskin? That one rug of hers must have begun to decay. He could smell putrefaction.

Or was it only that the old woman had started taking off her clothes? That was an unkind thought. But drat it, she'd probably never taken a bath in her life.

Then again, the smell might be coming from the cave. They'd been stepping back into the tunnel and employing one of the niches as a comfort station, since she wouldn't let them go out into the woods and they could hardly use a corner of the hut. Though maybe their hostess herself wouldn't have been so fussy.

Come to think of it, he'd heard some pretty feculent stories about what the plumbing had been like in those fairy tale castles the Stott kids' Aunt Matilda had no doubt filled their infant minds with. Why couldn't such places stay in storybooks? What if he got stuck in this unhygienic fantasy? What if he never got back to the college? What if he never saw Helen again?

If he were Torchyld, he could at least cry. As it was, he didn't even dare swear out loud for fear of embarrassing that pathetic old—Great jumping jehoshaphat! Why was she making those hideous grunting noises?

Thinking the woman must be in some kind of trouble, Peter opened the eyes he'd modestly shut when she began to undress. He hadn't expected to see anything pretty. He could never, never have anticipated what he saw.

She was naked now, her body turned toward him. One pair of withered breasts would have been enough to turn his stomach. This woman had five pairs, lined up on both sides of her torso like the dugs of an old sow.

She looked bigger without her clothes. Much bigger. Good God, she was growing before his eyes. Could that stuff she'd been burning be having a hallucinogenic effect on him? Or was the peasant face he'd thought so simple, so careworn, actually being transformed? Was the nose lengthening into a snout? Had the eyes become little dark rounds that flared red when the firelight hit them?

And the teeth! She'd seemed to have no teeth at all, supping up the broth from the trencher and gumming Stott's melted cheese off an acorn cake. Now the mouth showed great, pointed incisors and horribly tusklike canines. He didn't even want to imagine the bicuspids.

She was splashing some dark stuff on her ropy arms, smearing it around her frightful snout. He wondered what it could be. Then he knew, and wished to God he'd never eaten from that accursed cauldron.

This was no peasant. This was Cerridwen, or one of her litter, and the way she kept licking those foul chops as she bent over young Torchyld's magnificent body showed what those hideous teeth were for.

"Ye cave be where I store my food," she'd told them. She would sate her dreadful hunger on that great, handsome frame, then hang up the rest of them like sides of beef in a butcher's warehouse, to be dripped on with the stalactites until she got hungry again.

Well, Peter was damned if he'd let himself or any of his comrades provide chops and cutlets for that ten-titted horror. But how in Sam Hill was he going to stop her? She was enormous now, bigger than Stott, bigger than Torchyld; so big he couldn't see how the tiny hut held her.

Then he realized they weren't in any hut. They were still in the cave. The hut had been a mere contrivance of thatch and wattles: stage scenery for the pathetic old-woman act that had lulled them into feeling safe enough to get drunk on her hell-brew. No wonder she'd fed them that line about not venturing beyond the cowhide. They'd have found nothing outside but more rock. Great God, would they ever get out? Would it be kinder to let her kill them all quickly? No, damn it, such a death was unthinkable.

Cerridwen, or whatever she was, had gone on to Tim, curling her snout in scorn at his puny frame. She turned to Dan, nodding and cackling over his stately height and impressive poundage. Then she looked thoughtful.

"Perchance 'twould be wiser to save this one for a rainy day," she mused aloud. "He be comely of countenance"— Stott did in fact somewhat resemble a particularly majestic and distinguished porker—"and he be courtly in demeanor. 'Tis long since I last took a consort. Sometimes I find myself missing Lord Mochyn. But he did make a sumptuous pot roast. Ah, decisions, decisions. No matter, I can think about that later. First, to enjoy ye young giant Dwydd sent me. I suppose I ought to drop her a thank-you note. He will roast nicely. Or should I tear ye living flesh from ye quivering bones with my razor-sharp fangs, let ye blood roll down my chin, and hark with pleasure to his shrieks of agony until he hath nothing left to shriek with? As for that one in ye corner," she cast a disparaging glance at Peter, "not much to go to ye table with, but better than rabbit stew, methinks!"

Then at least it probably had been a rabbit in the pot. Peter found a tiny drop of comfort in that. Perhaps it was the last drop he'd ever have. Did the bitch have to keep licking her chops so avidly? Was there no way out of this nightmare?

Peter stole furtive glances from under his eyelashes, spying around for anything that might conceivably be used as a weapon. No use trying to tackle that monster with his bare hands. She'd have them chewed off to the armpits before he could get them around her throat. His only chance was in guile. He'd never felt more guileless in his life.

Then his glance fell on the harp Torchyld had flung into the corner behind the bench. It was no sort of weapon, but it was better than nothing. While the monstrous creature had her back to him, gloating over Torchyld, Peter snaked out his hand and grabbed the harp. It jangled. There was only one thing to do now, and he did it.

"A hog he would a-wooing go,

"Hi-ho, says Rowley."

Peter was no singer, he'd never twanged a harp before in his life, but that was beside the point. Bards were supposed to have the power of song over the birds of the air, the beasts of the field, the minds and the hearts of men. Did this thing have a mind, or a heart? No matter. At least he might distract her long enough for the others to wake up and make a run for it, though God only knew where they could run to. He sat up on his haunches, swept his hands back and forth across the strings to make as much noise as possible, and bellowed on.

"O bury me not on the lone prairee.

"These words came low and mournfullee

"From the pallid lips of a sow who lay

"On her dying bed at the close of day."

He couldn't be charming the hag, but he'd certainly managed to shake her aplomb. She stood staring at him through those mad, red eyes; her snout quivering, her jaw dropped to show rows of abominable, file-like teeth. He kept singing and strumming. As he played, he rose and backed slowly toward the cave mouth, praying his feet would locate a loose rock he might quickly scoop up and hurl. He'd been a pretty good shortstop for the Wheatfields Nine in his youth. The old wing still had enough juice in it to knock out a few of those God-awful teeth, anyway.

This was too slow. He struck up a livelier jangle and danced to the rhythm, bounding around in a wild jig that seemed to fascinate her more than the music.

"Git out the way, ol' Dan Tucker!
"Git out the way, ol' Dan Tucker!"

Why in hell didn't his companions wake up? He cavorted over toward the cave wall, still hoping to find something he could throw, but any rock he encountered had been glued to the floor by that eternally dripping mineral water.

Water! Peter scrooched down and managed to drag the hem of his robe through a puddle, danced back, and slapped the robe across the sleepers' faces, one after another. They groaned, stirred. He danced back and soaked his garment again, and again and again till he was ready to fall with exhaustion. Still the hag had made no move to attack. Maybe he had in fact managed to work an enchantment. She started clapping her blood-streaked hands, swaying in time to the music. It was revolting to watch all those yellow dugs flap to and fro, but better than being eaten. Then praise the Lord, Tim woke up.

"Pete, what the hell?" he grumbled.

"Oh, git out the way, ol' Tim Tucker," Peter caroled,

"Or you'll be goddamn sorry you stayed for supper!"

"Great Christ on a crutch!" Tim looked from his madly jigging friend to the naked, swaying, clapping hag. Then, incredibly, he started to laugh, leaped to his feet, and began dancing, too.

"Jee-hoshaphat, Pete, if you ain't the damnedest! Dan! Hey, Dan, wake up. We're having a hoedown. Swing it, Pete. Sashay left and all hands 'round. Whee! Haw, haw!"

Maybe it was hysteria. It could hardly have been anything else, but Peter began laughing, too. He twanged and stomped and ho-ho-ho'd, totally out of control. He slapped the hem of his wet robe back and forth across Dan Stott's face until at last their colleague sat up.

"Wherefore the levity, friends?"

That set them off again. Dan, normally the most decorous of swine experts, rose up to laugh and leap with them. At last they managed to rouse Torchyld.

"Oh, my head!" he groaned, then he realized what was going on and joined the roaring roisterers.

"I'faith, hag, ye knowest well how to maken merry. This be funnier than when I made Owain eat the boiled eels."

The only one not laughing was the hag. All that male guffawing appeared to terrify her as perhaps no threat of physical violence could have done. She was cowering away from them and beginning, Shandy thought, to shrink.

"Come on, old sow," he yelled boldly. "Put on your clothes and join the party."

Peter danced over and picked up the garment she'd thrown off in her ghastly transformation. "Phew, this is ripe. I'll wash it for you."

He sloshed the reeking rag through a pool in the cave floor, and flung it at her.

"Squee-ee-ee!"

As the sopping, cold cloth hit her, the sow sorceress squealed a horrendous squeal. Then came a mighty explosion. Loathsome fragments flew around them. A direful stench filled the air.

"Great balls of fire," yelled Tim. "What happened?"

"She brast," said Torchyld matter-of-factly. "Good show, druids."

"What do you mean, she brast?" Tim insisted. "Where is she?"

"Around," said Peter. "Let's get out of here. This place stinks like a bunkhouse full of lumberjacks."

Daniel Stott was inclined to stand and ruminate on what had occurred, but Peter hurried him off. "Come on, Dan. You can think on the way."

"On the way to where?" Tim wanted to know.

"I wish I knew. As far as I can tell, we're still inside the cave."

"Not for long," said Torchyld.

"How do you know?"

"It standeth to reason. Ye hag had firewood and herbs and a

fresh-killed rabbit. I be no great and wisdom-stuffed druid like ye, but to me these things grow not in caves."

"But she was a witch, or some damned thing," Peter argued. "Maybe she conjured them up."

"Conjured, hell," Tim snorted. "The kid's right. Come on, Pete, quit dithering. You're the one who said we'd better leave."

"I know I did. I'm only wondering if we'd better take some torches to light our way. Our ambulatory flashlight doesn't seem to be around."

"I be here." This was the prissy voice they recalled from their weary trek through the cave. "Only I fear I glow no more. I be disenchanted, ye see."

The voice's owner stepped forth from the cave. They found themselves faced by a man not more than four and a half feet tall. He was dressed only in a rude loincloth or kilt of something that looked like worn-out burlap, and his feet were bare. What hair he had was badly in need of a trim; his beard was so straggly it hardly seemed worth the bother of growing. He looked to be well on toward middle age, but that meant nothing, since middle age here could be anything. He was skinny and downtrodden-appearing. This was no doubt to be expected in a gone-out glow.

"She disembodied me so she wouldn't have to feed me," he was explaining. "I must say it feeleth good to be back in mine own shape, such as it be."

"You'll never be hung for your beauty, that's for sure," said Tim, rather pleased to have somebody in the group less physically prepossessing than himself. "Mind telling us who you are and how you got here?"

"What care we how he got here?" Torchyld interrupted with that suave courtesy they'd learned to expect from a king's great-nephew. "Can he guide us out?"

"Oh yes, no problem," said the ex-glow. "Just follow me, please. If ye don't mind joining hands—mine be a bit grubby, I fear—and making a chain, it will be easier for me to lead you without a light. I ken every puddle and pothole in this weary, weary cave."

"But why should we trust you?" Shandy demanded. "Look where you landed us last time."

"Ye be all-wise, great druid, and I be ye lowliest wretch that e'er groveled along a cave floor. I perceive now that I erred by not leaving ye and thy co-mates to perish in ye dark or be crushed by ye hogweed. I most humbly crave pardon."

"M'yes, neatly put. What were you before you got disembodied? A lawyer?"

"I was clerk to my liege, Lord Mochyn."

"The chap who became the—er—gentleman friend of that whatever-she-was?"

"She was a cruel enchantress, great druid. If she had a name, I wot it not. She spared my life and that of my liege lord only on condition that we do her every bidding. We were the last of a band of ten travelers who had been caught like yourselves by ye giant hogweed and herded into her clutches. By ye time she tracked us down, she had already eaten two and salted down ye others for her winter's store. Hence she was not enhungered, otherwise we had been devoured like them."

"How did you happen to be the last ones caught?"

"Lord Mochyn had fled into ye remote fastnesses of the cave, thinking to escape her fell design. I followed him as was my duty, so we were caught together. She made him her leman and me her guide, to lure ye unwary to her lair and save her ye bother of having to chase them through ye darksome caverns."

"I see. It never occurred to you to lead them elsewhere?"

"Nay, sire, I wot my responsibility to my employer."

"I see. You're not—er—working for anybody else now?"

"Not I, great druid. My liege be gone, ye enchantress be brast. At last I know what freedom meaneth. To be free is to be out of a job. Mayhap ye will allow me to guide ye out of ye cave on approval? Perchance, gin I give satisfaction, ye will then keep me in mind should an opening come up."

CHAPTER 7

Peter shrugged and took hold of the little man's hand. "Lead on, then. We can't stay here. What's your name, by the way?"

"Medrus, your druidity."

"All right, Medrus. Come along, everybody. We're moving out."

The three others, numb from the witch's brew they hadn't had time to sleep off as well as from their incredible awakening, clasped hands in turn and stumbled along behind. It wasn't very far to the real cave opening, perhaps a quarter of a mile, but it was tough going with no light whatever. Tim minded the trek most.

"Damn it, Medrus," he grumbled, "can't you even glimmer a little?"

Medrus couldn't, but he did keep up his running patter like Emma Woodhouse's neighbor, Miss Bates. "Prithee mind ye stalagmite here. Observe ye puddle."

Tim was still feeling the damp in his bones, the horror of their narrow escape from the hag, and a hangover the like of which he hadn't experienced since his late wife Jemima made him try her elderberry wine.

"How the hell do you expect us to observe what we can't even see?" he snapped.

After that, Medrus maintained a hurt silence until at last they emerged into bright sunshine. Then he collapsed, writhing on the ground and screaming, "Aagh! 'Tis not to be borne."

"Now what's eating you?" Tim snarled.

"It's the daylight," said Peter. "God knows how long the poor bugger's been crawling around inside that cave. He'll need a while to adjust."

"How long a while? Damn it, Pete, we can't lollygag around

here for the rest of our lives waiting for this pipsqueak's eye-balls to settle down."

"I myself would be content to lollygag awhile," said Daniel Stott, propping himself against a conveniently situated beech tree. "We might employ the interval in cogitation upon which direction we ought to proceed in when we resume our march."

"Straight to King Sfyn's castle," said Peter.

"But we can't," Torchyld howled. "We haven't found ye griffin yet. Gin I go back there without old Ffyff, they list to hurl me from ye parapets and boil me in oil. Or boil me in oil and then hurl me from ye parapets. I forget ye protocol. I feel not well."

"I'm tired myself," Peter admitted. "It's been a rough night. I move we find a good place to camp, and sack in for a while. Here, Medrus, sit up a minute. Let's see what we can do about those eyes."

He ripped a narrow strip off the hem of his still-sodden robe and bound it around the clerk's forehead. Then he plucked a few short, leafy twigs and thrust them under the headband so that the leaves hung down to serve as a primitive visor.

"There, that ought to help a little. Try opening your eyes for just a second at a time, until you begin to feel comfortable."

Medrus ventured a quick squint. "Gramercy, great and bountiful sir. Such munificence is astounding. Now gin I could only have some small morsel to eat. I have not tasted food since I entered ye cave with my liege, Lord Mochyn, in times agone, and I must say I begin to feel a trifle peckish."

At the word "food," Daniel Stott started up in alarm. "Dear me, this is indeed a parlous state of affairs. We are totally unprovisioned. Let us temporarily thrust aside our own dis-comforts and seek sustenance for this luckless wight. Medrus, would you settle temporarily for roots and berries in lieu of more substantial fare?"

"Marry, I would not," grumbled Torchyld. "Up and to ye hunt. Who hath my sword?"

"Great Scott," cried Peter, "haven't you?"

"Would I be asking if I had?"

"Then it must still be back in the cave, drat it. Why in hell couldn't you have hung on to it? Your sword was the only weapon we had, except Tim's golden sickle, and that won't cut hot butter."

"There's the harp," Tim wheezed. "Why don't you try charming a few partridges out of the trees, Peter? Give 'em one of your song-and-dance routines. God, that was funny."

He began to chortle at the memory. At once a shower of beechnuts dropped from the tree, pelting Tim on his bald head and caroming off his beard. Torchyld found this hilarious and laughed also, only to get zonked by an even heavier fall. At once he fell to cracking the fine, fat nuts in his fingers.

"Here, clerk," he said, handing Medrus the first handful of kernels. *"Noblesse oblige.* Chew them slowly, lest they give ye a bellyache."

"Thankee, noble bard," the clerk replied humbly. "I cannot chew other than slowly. I possess but two teeth, and they not in line with one another."

He began mumbling beechnuts while the others cracked and munched. Peter rapped his nuts cleanly with a rock and got out a perfect kernel every time. Daniel Stott carefully and deliberately opened a fair-sized heap, then settled down to concentrated mastication. Torchyld went at the job with such energy that he was soon surrounded by crumbled shells and squashed kernels, which he scooped up and gave to Medrus.

"Eat these, clerk. They will save those two teeth some grinding."

Tim cracked and ate a few, then said, "Oh hell, that's too much like work." He'd never been a big eater, anyway.

Peter soon lost interest in the beechnuts, too. He gazed up into the branches, his brow furrowed in thought. After a while, he crowed. "Gentlemen, I think I've got it."

"Whate'er it be, I want some," said Torchyld.

"You have all you want right now."

"All of what? Fleas? Nay, druid, of those I have more than I want."

"You and me both," growled Tim. "That cursed sheepskin must have been crawling with 'em. I move we find ourselves a swimming hole and take a bath."

"A what?" said Medrus.

"A bath. Like when you get into water and wash yourself all over."

"For what purpose, great archdruid?"

"To get the dirt off, dang it."

"Ah. Vast is thy wisdom, though strange thy customs. Prithee, sir bard, be there any more nuts?"

"Be my lowly guest."

Torchyld considerately mashed another handful for him. "I might perchance also give ye some of whatever else I have in such abundance, gin I knew what it be."

"Very funny," said Peter, and laughed.

His wasn't a particularly hearty laugh, barely more than a snicker, but it fetched another small shower of beechnuts. "See," he said, "it happens every time."

"That nuts fall from trees?" the young giant scoffed. "Vast indeed is thy wisdom, druid. What else can a nut do?"

"It happens whenever we laugh, is what I'm driving at. Don't you get it? Laughter, that's our most effective weapon. Remember what happened to the sorceress?"

"She brast."

"I know she brast. I've still got a few reminders scattered over my nightshirt. I'm all for the swimming hole, too, Tim. But what I mean is, she brast after we'd begun to laugh. Don't you remember? First she began to cower away and shrink."

"But it wasn't till you heaved that wet rag at her that she brast," Tim argued. "Busted. Whatever the hell she did. I say it was the cold water that finished her off."

"I incline toward Timothy's thesis," said Dan Stott. "I believe I mentioned before that in the case of the trifids, water proved to be the effective dissolving agent. A similar incident was described in a book to which my daughters were much addicted during their formative years. I must say I found the narrative a trifle farfetched in spots, though the character of the lion was subtly drawn. In any event, this took place in a region known as Oz, when a child named Dorothy effected the demise of a wicked witch by pouring a bucketful of water over her. Hence we have well-documented evidence that witches recoil from the threat of water."

"She'd already recoiled before I sloshed her," Shandy insisted. "I grant you the cold water may have triggered the final explosion, but it would be unscientific to overlook the preliminary effect of the laughter."

Dan pondered awhile, then essayed an experimental chortle. He got one beechnut and a much put-out starling.

"Ye tree knew ye didn't really mean it," said Torchyld.

"You fooled the starling, though," said Tim.

The bird gave him a dirty look and flew off.

"The salient fact," Stott decided, "is that I did in fact get a result. This bears out Peter's argument and means we are less defenseless than we might have supposed. He who can laugh in the face of adversity is in sober fact thrice-armed, it appears. I find myself greatly heartened by this knowledge."

"Urrgh," said Torchyld. "I still wish I had my sword. Mayhap I should go back and get it."

"Mayhap you shouldn't," said Peter. "I have a feeling that would be a remarkably stupid thing to do. Would you settle for a quarterstaff?"

"A what?"

"A long stick, suitable for prodding and lambasting."

"Oh, a *ffon.* That be a peasant's weapon. And forsooth, who careth?"

Torchyld leaped to his feet and went on the prowl. It wasn't long before he found a *ffon* to his liking, about six feet long and as big around as Dan Stott's arm. Peter thought it more suited for tossing the caber than hand-to-hand combat, but he didn't say so.

"Might ye rest of us not equip ourselves with *ffons,* too, if I may be so bold as to offer ye suggestion?" Medrus ventured.

With his eyes now fully open and all those beechnuts under his kilt, the clerk looked a shade less weedy, though still a wretchedly inferior specimen. His suggestion was sensible enough, though, so they all began equipping themselves according to their tastes. Tim chose a sturdy branch about three feet long with a knob at the top, which he could use as a war club or a walking stick as occasion offered. Medrus followed his example on a punier scale to befit his rank and stature. Dan Stott managed to find a tall staff with the top looped over to suggest a shepherd's crook or a bishop's crozier.

Dan did look remarkably like a bishop, or some such august personage, in that long white robe and headdress, with the fillet of gold across his hairless brow. No wonder the hag had fallen for him, Peter thought. He himself aroused Torchyld's derision by selecting not one but three sticks: short, straight, and strong; none of them bigger around than a plant stick. He also gathered up a few feathers the starling had shed when it fell out of the tree, and stowed them in a fold of his robe.

Peter was also still carrying the harp, which Torchyld appeared to have handed over to him on the strength of his stellar performance back in the cave. Now he hoisted it back over his shoulder and jerked his head forward.

"What do you say, men? Let's start hunting for water. I want a drink and I want a bath. And I want to wash this filthy damned burnous I'm wearing. And then I want a nap. The rest of you at least managed to get a little sleep last night. I never closed my eyes."

"It still amazeth me, noble druid, that ye alone were not felled by Gwrach's magic potion," Medrus remarked.

"That so?" Shandy gave him a narrow look. "It amazeth me that you know her name all of a sudden. Back there a while, you said you didn't."

"Great sir, I durst not then utter it. Mayhap I should not have dursted now."

"You mean the evil that she did lives after her?"

"I cannot say. I only fear."

"Laugh it off," Tim snorted. "Mayhap you can snicker up a stack of buckwheat cakes. Let's strike downhill, Pete. We're more apt to find water on low ground. Besides, I'd rather go down than up."

"Right, Tim."

Peter was growing deeply concerned for his old buddy. Tim was a tough old rooster for his years, but he wouldn't be able to stand much more of this. He'd keep going till he dropped, of course, rather than admit he was done in, but how soon was he going to drop? It was an ineffable relief to come upon an open, grassy bank with a genteel creek meandering through. Better still, the sun they'd seen back at the cave mouth and hardly been able to glimpse since then in the thick forest was warming the grass nicely.

They all crouched at the water's edge and took long drinks. Then Peter remarked, "Great day for the wash," stripped off his soiled robe, and waded in with it over his arm, leaving the harp, the feathers, and his three sticks on the bank.

"How's the water, Pete?" Tim asked him.

"Great. Come on in, everybody. Good for what ails you."

Torchyld plunged in as a warrior should, splashing and wallowing and insisting it wasn't a bit cold once you got ducked. Tim followed, then Dan Stott, still wearing his white robe and looking a bit like Moby Dick. At last Medrus waded in ankle deep and dithered there moaning until Torchyld picked him up by the ankles and pitched him in head first. Once over the initial shock, he paddled around like a puppy and put on airs about his bravery in entering this foreign element.

Without soap, they couldn't get themselves or their clothes really clean. They did their best, however, all except Medrus, who couldn't seem to grasp the principle of washing. At last, refreshed and at least semipurified, they came ashore, spread out their garments to dry on the grass, and eased themselves down to rest. Before long, Torchyld caught the older men yawning.

"How can ye sleep?" he chided. "Men on ye march drowse not without first setting a sentry."

He sounded as if he hoped they'd talk him out of the idea, but nobody did so he had to sit alone listening to Tim snore, Dan snuffle, and Medrus emit strange whuffling noises like a dog dreaming of chasing a rabbit. Peter merely slept, or tried to until he felt himself being prodded in the ribs.

"Hist, druid," whispered the self-appointed sentry. "Something cometh."

"What cometh?" Peter growled back. "Why couldn't you wake somebody else?"

"Because ye old one and ye fat one outrank me, and ye scrawny runt I trust not. Behold."

Peter sat up and beheld. "Well, I'll be jiggered," he exclaimed when he'd spotted the object bobbing toward them down the stream. "A floating washtub. Is that what they call a coracle?"

The vessel looked to be about the size and shape of his grandmother's zinc bathtub, woven basketwise of osiers or some such withy material, and covered with stretched cowhide. Shandy had seen pictures of them, but had never really believed anybody would voluntarily set out from shore in so flimsy a craft.

"Who's in it?" he asked Torchyld. "Can you see?"

"I see nobody. It floateth high on ye water, yet acts as if it were being steered."

Torchyld waded out into the stream, his staff held ready just in case. In a moment, the coracle had bobbed close enough for him to look inside.

"Empty," he announced. "Unless there be a disembodied boatman."

"That be entirely possible."

It was Medrus who'd spoken. Their talk had wakened him and Timothy Ames, who were both eyeing the coracle with keen interest.

"Bring it ashore, son," Tim called out.

Before Torchyld could obey, the little boat of itself changed course and swerved in the direction of Tim's voice.

"It obeyeth ye archdruid," laughed the king's great-nephew. "Come hither, boat." He waded ashore. Sure enough, the coracle bobbed along behind him, into the shallows next to the bank.

Now that he could get a good look at it, Peter saw that the wicker frame was skillfully woven and the hide covering shrunk so tight to it that it made a dry, light, and probably efficient craft. It would be tippy and cranky to steer until you got the hang of it, but could be rowed or paddled without much effort.

He'd heard Welsh fishermen would take their coracles out off the coast in all weathers. He'd hate to try that himself, but on a meandering creek like this one, the little boat might be at least a temporary answer to Tim's fatigue. The problem was, how could they all fit in? The coracle looked as if it would founder under the weight of Torchyld and Dan alone, not to mention trying to squeeze the others in around them.

Maybe it would be possible to make a rope of vines or strips from their robes, and float the coracle along with Tim and that poor shrimp Medrus in it while the rest towed from the bank. That was, of course, provided the stream flowed in the direction they wanted to take. He asked Torchyld. The young giant only stared at him.

"Dost expect me to know? I thought ye did."

"But how the hell—" Peter caught himself. He'd forgotten he was supposed to be infallible. While he was wondering how to save face, Dan Stott blinked, opened his eyes without undue haste, and slowly sat up.

"Ah," he remarked. "The boat has arrived."

"Cripes, Dan, you sound as if you've been expecting it," said Tim.

"Let us rather say that I am not surprised. Such craft are frequent manifestations in the vignettes of local history to which I alluded earlier. It has come to take us on the next leg of our journey."

"The hell it has. Where's that?"

"We shall no doubt be informed when we get there."

Stott arose, picked up his now dry robe, shook it free of lounging grasshoppers, and put it on. He adjusted the gold fillet around his head-covering, made a discreet trip behind a convenient tree, came back, and announced, "I am ready."

"You're actually going to ride in that boat?" Tim demanded.

"We all are, are we not?"

"How the hell can we? The damn thing's no bigger than my Aunt Winona's old sitz bath."

"I suggest that Sir Torchyld and I, because of our greater weight and girth, take the bow and stern respectively. If you and Medrus sit side by side in front of me and Peter takes his place between you two and Sir Torchyld, we should be able to trim the boat adequately."

"Trim, hell! She'll be slam on the bottom with all hands before we can get our rumps planted."

"I believe not. Such an occurrence has not cropped up in any of the literature sent by my sister Matilda. Passengers are merely wafted over the rippling waters while gentle breezes fan their temples. Sometimes ethereal music is heard, sometimes not."

"Sometimes there's a rudder and sail, or a pair of oars, or some damn thing to navigate with, isn't there?" Tim insisted.

"Such accoutrements are not strictly necessary," Dan informed him. "The boat is guided by mysterious forces."

"What forces?"

"That detail is never explained, possibly to enhance the atmosphere of mystery. One merely trusts. Sir Torchyld, if you and I get in simultaneously from opposite sides, I believe we shall thus minimize the danger of capsizing."

Tim snickered meanly. "Some trust. Go ahead, Dan. We can all use a good laugh. Might bring down something else to eat."

"There is, as I rather anticipated, a lunch basket in the boat," Dan replied mildly, setting one large foot in the flimsy craft and pulling the other in after it.

Torchyld stepped briskly aboard at the same time. Shandy watched for the coracle to founder. To his astonishment, it appeared to ride almost as high in the water as before. Stott and Torchyld were now passing chicken legs, jam tarts, and bunches of grapes back and forth like two ladies at a tea party. Medrus moaned.

"Might I not go in ye coracle, great druids? It be so long, so very long—"

"Oh, what the hell? Come on. Here, boys, take your staves."

Peter got Tim and Medrus stowed aboard, then he climbed over the gunwale himself. It was a tight squeeze, even with his knees up under his chin, but at least he got his jam tart before Torchyld ate them all.

"Now who's going to shove off?" Tim demanded with his mouth full of chicken. "Assuming we can get off at all."

"We are already afloat," Dan told him, reaching calmly for the last drumstick.

Lo and behold, they were. The coracle had moved out into the middle of the stream and the mysterious forces were buckling down to serious business. They were none of them comfortable but the chicken was juicy, the fruit was sweet, and for drink they had only to dangle their cupped hands over the side and scoop up the cold, clear river water.

The water was remarkably good in this enchanted land. Peter only hoped it wasn't laden with typhus germs. Probably it wasn't. That would come with modern progress. He drank some more and rubbed his wet hands across his face to wash off the traces of his picnic lunch. He needed a shave. So did Dan. Tim hadn't shaved in years, and he doubted whether Medrus had ever shaved at all; though Torchyld's blond mustache was at least decently trimmed.

There was something to be said for beards. He'd have one himself, no doubt, before they got out of this mess. A gray one. If they ever did. He sighed and tried to find a more comfortable position. It wasn't easy, sitting scrunched up on this blasted wickerwork. The crew's backsides would look like a plate of waffles by the time they disembarked. Why couldn't the mysterious forces have laid on a bigger boat? And a few cushions?

Nice of them to have thought of the lunch, though. Too bad there wasn't more of it. The forces must have been expecting a smaller party. At least they were moving the boat along at a good clip. It was rolling slightly now. Medrus was beginning to look a bit green.

"Lean over the side and wet your head if you start to feel funny," Peter told the clerk.

"Great druid, I dare not move."

"You'd damn well better move if you're going to be sick," Tim growled.

Maybe Medrus did and maybe he didn't. Peter couldn't stay awake to find out. The warm sun, the gentle breeze wafting as predicted about their temples, the rocking motion of the boat, were lulling him and the rest back to sleep. Torchyld, who'd so gallantly kept watch while they were napping back on the riverbank, was already snuffling gently, murmuring "Syglinde" every so often and looking surprisingly angelic. Dan Stott was probably asleep, too. It was hard to tell, with Dan.

Medrus had dropped off when Shandy roused himself to check, and was making those whimpering noises again. Poor bastard, Peter thought muzzily. God alone knew what horrors he'd been subjected to by that monstress Gwrach, aside from the trauma of being disembodied. Or what he'd gone through beforehand, if it came to that. Lord Mochyn couldn't have been the world's greatest employer, either. Any human being who'd be willing to engage in sexual congress (Peter was something of a prude in certain ways) with a creature like that deserved to wind up in the soup.

He didn't feel so well, himself. Maybe the chicken had been slightly off from sitting out in the sun in that picnic basket. Not that he'd had enough of it to matter.

And that was still an interesting point to consider. He'd had no previous experience of enchantments, but it did seem as if whatever power was engineering this excursion could have provided more adequate accommodations. Unless the coracle was just some kind of ferryboat that drifted around looking for business and took anybody who came along, regardless. Or unless the mysterious forces had been expecting a smaller group, as he'd wondered before.

They mightn't have counted on Medrus. He'd been sort of an accidental addition, though not a big enough one to count for much. It was Torchyld who really made the difference. And it was Torchyld whom the hags had been out to get. That old bat Dwydd had made two attempts on his life already that Peter knew about: once when she'd disenchanted his sword and presented him with those two quite possibly poisoned biscuits as he was on his way to kill the wyvern; and the second when she'd swiped the griffin and the girl to create a situation that would send him into the clutches of Gwrach, weaponless and distraught over his sudden demotion from hero to villain. Gwrach herself had talked of sending Dwydd a thank-you note for the lovely dinner, so there could be no doubt the whole thing was a put-up job.

Torchyld's thinking he'd been switched by magic from a

warrior to a bard was nonsense, of course. If there'd really been any enchantment, he would presumably have been given some bardly attributes instead of just a harp and a heave-ho. Torchyld was no more a bard than Peter Shandy was. Less of one, in fact. Peter didn't particularly enjoy recalling the events of the previous night, but nobody could deny his first go at bardship had been a bang-up performance.

It appeared that Torchyld, unlike the college president he so oddly resembled, wasn't very bright. No, that wasn't so at all. Torchyld had brains enough when he chose to use them, if his own account of how he'd killed the wyvern was true. He was—unawakened, that was it. A child of his time, no doubt. This was an era, and a country, where strange things happened.

Shandy had to believe that. He'd seen it with Medrus; he'd seen it, God help him, with Gwrach. He'd seen the hogweed growing before his eyes. And Tim's eyes, and Dan's eyes. Right now he was sitting in a boat that was certainly moving as though some unseen intelligence was guiding it, even if it had been ordinary human hands that packed the lunch and set the coracle adrift.

Torchyld must have seen a fair amount of this sort of thing. He couldn't help believing in enchantments because he knew they happened. Therefore, he might well be conditioned to believe in enchantments that hadn't really happened at all. The young fellow simply hadn't yet learned to separate the abra from the cadabra.

Would he ever get a chance to learn? Somebody was going to a lot of fuss and bother to get him killed. Was it Dwydd, acting on her own, or was the resident hag just doing a favor for some member of the king's household? And why would one of them want him dead? Was it because of his girl, or his wealth, or because his father who'd been eaten by a garefowl had been the rightful king and Torchyld was the true heir to the throne? God, Peter wished he could stretch his legs.

The sun was bothering him now, going down and sending oblique rays straight into his eyes. So they were heading due west, if that meant anything. Peter draped a fold of his robe across his eyes to shut out the glare. That was better. Soothing. Restful. He'd just keep his eyes shut a minute longer to ease their smarting.

CHAPTER 8

Peter slept. He couldn't tell for how long, but when he woke, the moon was either coming up or going down. Down, he thought. As Huck Finn would say, it felt late and it smelt late. A long time since he'd read that flawed masterpiece. Too long. Well, there wasn't much he could do about it now.

Tim and the others were still pounding their ears. At least they hadn't been eaten by sea serpents or invaded by water voles. The little boat was still clipping along at a lively rate. Gradually, that fact began to worry him.

When they met, Torchyld had been banished from King Sfyn's castle for less than a day. He hadn't had any great head of steam on when Shandy first saw him; he'd been too burdened by his weight of woe to have put many leagues between himself and his vanished bride-to-be. Fifteen or twenty miles at the outside, say, and probably nearer ten.

After they'd met Tim and Dan, they probably hadn't gone any distance at all. They'd wasted time palavering on the path, then the hogweed had chased them into that cave. Once inside, it seemed as if they'd traveled endlessly, but in all likelihood it hadn't been more than a mile or two. Nor had they covered a great deal of ground before they'd stopped to rest after their hair-raising night, and found the boat. Or the boat had found them.

If they were floating in the general direction of King Sfyn's castle, therefore, they ought to be making port any time now. If not, they were being taken a good deal farther out of their way than they wanted to go.

It was all very well for Dan Stott to talk blandly about being assisted on the next leg of their journey. Shandy had little faith in *The Wizard of Oz* as a travel guide. He wished to Christ he'd thought to fetch along something they could use as a paddle. They did have their staves, and a devilish nuisance these were turning out to be in so tiny a craft, but the staves would be of no use unless they got close enough inshore to pole. The boat seemed to catch his thought, and took a sudden skip that sent them out into the middle of what Peter, now that his eyes were accustomed to the darkness, could see was no longer a stream but a good-sized lake.

What was the use of worrying? Obviously he wasn't in control here. He didn't know who was, or what, or why, or how. The boat must not have been sent to drown them; it could have managed that any time these past several hours. The only sensible thing for him to do was relax and enjoy the ride.

Relax, forsooth! Peter could barely manage to wiggle his eyebrows, let alone take a decent stretch to get the kinks out. How in tunket did the rest of the boys manage to sleep so soundly? And why did that twerp Medrus have to keep making those confounded noises?

Anybody can be noble and heroic in a real crisis. It's when you're in a situation where there's nothing much you can do, when you get a cramp in your left gastrocnemius, when you didn't get enough supper and you start brooding on that pint you never got to drink, that real fortitude is called for. It was low and mean and rotten to take umbrage when the offender meant no offense; nevertheless, if Peter Shandy could have got a foot untangled, he would have found exquisite relief in kicking Medrus to shut him up.

Perhaps Medrus, like the coracle, had a knack for intercepting thought waves. He slumped forward so that his scurfy head was all but resting on Shandy's knees, and stopped whimpering. Peter was about to try nudging him back, if it could be done without upsetting the boat, when he realized something was going on. Medrus was fumbling under his, Shandy's, robe.

Furious, Peter was ready to risk a shipwreck by belting him one when Medrus straightened up, raised something to his mouth, and began to gnaw. Now what had the little bastard got hold of? Peter sniffed and realized it must be a chicken leg he'd cunningly stashed in the bottom of the coracle for a late-night snack. Sneaky but understandable. One could hardly expect much in the way of high-minded morality from a person with his background. Still it was irksome. Peter was in a mood to be irked, no doubt. Drat it, how far was this pestiferous boat going to take them?

Medrus had finished his surreptitious repast. He must have gnawed halfway through the bone before, with obvious reluctance, he dropped it overboard and licked his fingers like a cat. Poor bugger, he had a big hollow to fill. A few beechnuts and what little he'd had from the picnic basket couldn't have gone far toward assuaging the kind of hunger the ex-clerk must have built up during his disembodiment. Peter told himself so and knew he should be ashamed for having to, but he still felt annoyed. He was sorry they'd acquired Medrus. He hoped he wouldn't be sorrier before this trip was over.

If it ever was. He tried to get back to sleep but found himself only napping by fits and starts, jerking awake to feel yet another crick in his neck or his back or his knee or his big toe. The night was a million years long. Dawn would never come. They'd drift on and on, getting stiffer and stiffer, finally withering away like dried-up kernels in last year's walnuts. On this happy thought he fell at last into a sound sleep, and woke to find the boat gliding up to a stone jetty at the foot of a towering castle.

"Wake up, everybody," he caroled. "We're going ashore."

"Huh?" Tim sat up as straight as he could manage, and rubbed his eyes. "Where are we?"

"I don't know, but we're somewhere," Peter told him. "Recognize this castle, Torchyld? It's not King Sfyn's?"

"Nay, I ken it not." Torchyld yawned. "No matter. They will give us a banquet."

"What makes you so sure?"

"Have to, in sooth. That be ye rule of etiquette. 'Tis unmannerly to slaughter us before they feed us. Even ye sorceress in ye cave knew that."

"True enough, she did. But—er—it's not the general custom to kill the guests after the meal, is it?"

"Oh no. They be more like to want to marry us off to their

ugly daughters," Torchyld replied, gloom settling over what could be seen of his countenance as he thought of all those unwed female cousins back home, not to mention his also unwed and now possibly mislaid Syglinde.

"Well, Dan and I are already married and you're betrothed," Shandy told him cheerily. "That leaves 'em only Tim and Medrus as prospects."

"Mayhap we had best not say so until we see how lies ye land. Who be I, druid?"

"Who—er, um, yes, I see what you mean. Perhaps for the time being, you'd better remain an apprentice bard."

"But I wot not of making poetry."

"That's right, you wotn't. You're still—er—learning the business and not allowed to perform in public yet. I'll do any barding that's necessary. Well, well, here's our welcoming committee."

Peter was none too easy in his mind about the men marching down to meet the boat. He felt a trifle less anxious, though, when he saw there wasn't a drawn weapon among them. Those few who did carry spears looked, from their tin soldier poses, to be doing so merely for ceremonial purposes. Peter waited until the boat had drifted within hailing distance, then tried an experimental, "Ahoy."

"They speak in strange tongues," he could hear one remarking to another.

"Drat it, what was I supposed to say?" Peter muttered to Torchyld.

"Ye might'st have tried 'hail.' "

"All right then, hail. Hail, hail, the gang's all here."

"What the hail do we care?" Tim chimed in. "Tell 'em to put on the coffeepot and bring on the mules to haul us out of this goddamn tub. I think my back's broken."

"Mine also," said Daniel Stott, coming to life without undue haste. "Do I gather we have attained our hitherto unknown destination?"

"It's still unknown at the moment," Peter told him, "but I guess this is as far as the boat goes."

Even now they were bobbing up to the jetty and eager hands

were reaching out to secure the coracle. Peter tried another hail and was answered by a veritable hailstorm.

"Hail to thee, blithe spirits," he finished off the chorus. "May we come ashore?"

"Welcome. Welcome, dammit."

The fattest and best-dressed of the group, a middle-aged man of medium height with sharp little blue eyes and gray hair, bustled forward rubbing his hands. "Happy to have ye aboard. Steady ye boat there, louts. Help our distinguished visitors out. Be ye bards or druids, honored sirs?"

"Some of each," Peter told him. "This venerable personage is Archdruid Timothy Ames, and this is Assistant Archdruid Daniel Stott. I'm Boss Bard Peter Shandy, this is Apprentice Bard Torchyld, and this chap in the sawed-off petticoat is Medrus, whom we found in a cave temporarily employed as a disembodied glow. He tells us he was once clerk to a Lord Mochyn. You wouldn't happen to have been acquainted with Lord Mochyn, by any chance?"

"Mochyn?" The head of the greeting party scratched his somewhat unkempt gray beard. "Ye name soundeth familiar, but I can't seem to place him. 'Twill come to me, sooner or later. I be Lord Ysgard and these be my sons: Yfor, Yfan, Yorich, Huw, Hywell, and Hayward. My steward be around here somewhere. Degwel! Hoy, Degwel! Shake a leg."

"I be here, my liege. I was but instructing some of ye minions to run and put another trencherful of boiled eels on ye banqueting board. No doubt our distinguished guests will wish to break their fast without delay."

"We shall be honored to sit at Lord Ysgard's board," said Peter, "and we thank you, Steward Degwel, for the boiled eels. Are we also indebted to you for sending this coracle to pick us up?"

"Nay, great bard, ye coracle be none of my doing. I would have chosen a vessel better suited to ye size of ye company."

"Degwel wotteth his stuff," said Lord Ysgard. "But come, come, ye must be famished. Have a good trip?"

"We got here," grunted Tim, hoisting himself out of the boat with the help of two of Lord Ysgard's stalwart sons. They were all tall and broad in the beam, all black-haired, black-eyed, and rosy-cheeked. Nice boys, they looked to be. Probably run to fat in later years if they took after their old man.

Where was Mrs. Ysgard? Peter wondered if it was the custom for the ladies of the house to keep out of sight until the men had got a chance to examine the moral principles of any newcomer. It did seem odd that not even a serving maid was sticking her head out from around the donjon keep to get a squint at the newcomers.

When they entered the castle, they still didn't see a woman. Nor were any present at the banqueting board when they entered the great hall, which in truth wasn't so great, though of course they weren't about to say so. When the five of them, Medrus below the salt and Torchyld down among the younger sons, refraining from voicing his displeasure only because Shandy kept giving him stern looks, took their places with Lord Ysgard, his family, the steward, and assorted members of the lordly household, there was barely room for the minions to squeeze through with the trenchers and the wolfhounds to forage behind the benches. Shandy could see why the Welsh had taken to breeding corgis.

Lord Ysgard kept up a hospitable flow of small talk while the ex-voyagers made up for lost mealtimes. Boiled eels weren't at all bad, Peter found. Daniel Stott was thoughtfully and painstakingly demolishing a trencherful singlehanded, while the six sons of Lord Ysgard, no mean trenchermen themselves, gazed upon him with awe and reverence. Peter did wish there were something other than ale to drink, and not even halfway palatable ale at that, but at least it helped the eels down.

The hall was a strangely cheerless place, Shandy thought. It wasn't too badly kept, he supposed; but there was no ease, no grace, not even any color to speak of, barring the florid face of Lord Ysgard. It wasn't homey. The master and his company were doing their best to be hospitable, but they simply didn't know how.

Torchyld was noticing. At first he looked puzzled. Then he asked, "Where be thy ladies, Lord Ysgard?"

"Be it meet for an apprentice bard to address so personal a

question to our liege?" Degwel inquired of an eel he was about
to eat.

"Oh yes," said Peter before Torchyld could retort in his own
fashion. "He is himself of noble birth."

"Then prithee, why be he apprenticed to a bard? No offense,
of course."

"And none taken," Peter replied sweetly. "Far be it from me
to castigate you in verse of mystic power just for asking a civil
question. Torchyld is apprenticed to me because he is under
enchantment and I happened to have an opening for an enchanted apprentice at the moment. When my colleagues and I
get through disenchanting him, he will resume his rightful
guise and you will be proud to have had the opportunity of—er
—splitting eels with him. Therefore, you may be pleased to
recall that you accorded him due respect now. With all respect
to yourself, of course."

Degwel glared at the eel and said nothing. Shandy turned to
their host.

"Lord Ysgard, I expect you and your people are wondering
how so distinguished a group as we are happen to be wandering loose around the country like a band of gypsies. Frankly, so
are we. The fact of the matter is, we've been having an adventure."

"An adventure?" A murmur of excitement went around the
board. "Wilt sing of ye adventure, noble bard?" asked Hywell,
or possibly Hayward.

"M'well, I haven't had time to put it into verse yet," Peter
answered. "Would you be satisfied with a mere telling?"

"In sooth, a mere telling would suit us fine. Poetry be always
such a bother to figure out."

"He hath a brain easily strained," said the brother next to
him. "Tell on, O bard. How cometh it ye and these venerable
druids have gone a-venturing together?"

"The druids and I are old comrades," Shandy began. "We
come from a great distance and how we traveled is a mystery
not meet for young ears like yours to hear."

This sort of thing wasn't so tough, once you fell into the way of it. "Suffice it to say we arrived in the country of King Sfyn—"

"King Sfyn? Can it be possible?" They were pointing at Torchyld and nudging each other. Shandy gave them an indulgent look and went on with his saga.

As Helen often said, Peter did have a way with words. Perhaps he had really been a bard in some transmigration or reincarnation or other. He'd have to check it out with Dan Stott sometime. Anyway, his yarn lost nothing and in fact gained a good deal in the telling. He extracted each last shred of dramatic value from the hogweed, from the perilous journey through the cave, from the mysterious glow that had guided them. Medrus became quite a hero down at the far end of the table. Peter described the encounter with Gwrach, using every adjective he could dredge from his early perusals of E. A. Poe and H. P. Lovecraft. When he got to the part where she brast, a wild cheer went up around the banqueting hall and Lord Ysgard bellowed for the drinking horn.

"Ye shall judge if our liquor be as potent as that of the dread sorceress. Eh, great archdruid?"

"Cripes, Pete, what am I supposed to do now?" muttered Tim. "Another drinking bout like that last one would send me six feet under."

"Then tell him you have to go and perform some secret rites," Peter suggested. "They must have a chapel in the castle."

"I can't go performing secret rites in some stranger's chapel. I couldn't do it in my own, if I had one. I don't know any secret rites. I never even joined the Odd Fellows."

"So make believe you're under a vow to abstain from strong drink until you've finished disenchanting Torchyld."

"Ale doesn't count?"

"How can it? You've already swilled a quart or two."

As Dan Stott's head was strong and his capacity great enough for a brace of druids, Lord Ysgard was not offended by Tim's vow of abstinence. He was as eager as the rest of them to see Torchyld disenchanted and his true identity revealed, though he was trying not to show it. His dignity seemed to be a kind of greased pig on which Lord Ysgard kept at best a precarious and spasmodic hold.

CHAPTER 9

The liquor was potent, all right. After the horn had gone around once or twice, Peter felt emboldened to say, "You still haven't introduced us to Lady Ysgard."

"Alas!"

He must have said the wrong thing with a vengeance. Not only Lord Ysgard but every member of his family and staff fell to weeping.

"I'm dreadfully sorry," Peter stammered. "I didn't realize you were still mourning her loss."

"It be not my wife," sniffled his lordship. "She ran off with a wandering minstrel many years agone. It be everybody. There be not a lady nor a maid or e'en a serving wench left in ye castle or ye village or all ye country around."

"Good God, what happened to them?"

"They be abducted by ye lecherous monster King Sfyn."

"King Sfyn be no monster," shouted Torchyld. "What ye hell would he go around abducting women for? He hath more women around him than he can handle already."

"Aye," cried the sons in a growling chorus. "Our women!"

"That be to say," explained Huw, who was evidently more articulate than the rest of the pack, "ye women we might have if King Sfyn's men hadn't got to them first. What happened was, there used to be this wyvern that would fly around King Sfyn's kingdom grabbing up maidens and devouring them. So they began to run short of maidens over there. So they came and got ours."

"It was disgusting," said Degwel. "Ye hussies would line up in rows outside the castle walls with their hair in braids and their lunches all packed, just waiting for some swashbuckling scoundrel from Sfynfford to come galloping over and abduct them."

"I gave strict orders against rape and ravishment," snarled Lord Ysgard, "but they flouted me, dammit. Hell of a note, being flouted by a lord's own damsels. Soon as they heard the wyvern had been killed, they began washing their necks and trimming their toenails to get ready for ye next raiding party. Claimed it was livelier over in Sfynfford. Ingrates!"

"We tried to organize a squad of our own to go and abduct some of them back," said Yfor gloomily, "but we could not get it together. Ye trouble is, nobody can find anything any more. When we had women around, they always kenned by some kind of instinct where ye'd parked your lance or shield or gyves or corselet or whatever. And they'd shine them up for ye, and comb ye nits out of thine hair so ye wouldn't go crazy with ye itch when ye put on thy helmet. Damn it, I want mine old nanny!"

He began to bawl again. Around him, the chorus of wails rose in sympathy.

"And you say they're every one of them over at Sfynfford now?" said Shandy, raising his voice to make himself heard above the din. "Dash it, quit that infernal yowling a minute, can't you? Give a man a chance to think."

In the hope of quelling the tumult, he picked up the harp and gave them a chorus of "I want a girl just like the girl that married dear old Dad." This, he realized too late, was an undiplomatic choice as it must inevitably remind Lord Ysgard of Lady Ysgard and the traveling minstrel. He switched to "Wouldst Could I but Kiss Thy Hand, O Babe," which struck a more responsive chord.

As the sobs quieted down to sighs of yearning, he remarked, "King Sfyn has several granddaughters, does he not, assistant bard? All single and all beautiful. I repeat, all beautiful," he added when he saw Torchyld's lip begin to curl.

"Imogene be not so bad," Torchyld admitted. "If ye likest fat brunettes."

The entire company voted unanimously in favor of fat brunettes.

"On ye other hand, if ye have a preference for skinny redheads, there be Guinevere."

They all expressed a willingness to prefer skinny redheads, given the opportunity. They were ready to prefer whomever they could get. The problem was, how to go about the getting.

Shandy vetoed the mere notion of a raiding party.

"Obviously you can't beat the Sfynffordians at abduction. What you must do is try a different approach. I'd recommend a diplomatic mission."

"A what?"

"A social call, if you prefer. Get yourselves slicked up in your Sunday go-to-meetings, take some nice presents, and go to call on the ladies. Tell them the fame of their beauty has spread far and wide, and you came to feast your eyes on so much amalgamated pulchritude."

"All of them together cannot—" Torchyld began. Shandy shut him up in a hurry.

"As you were saying, though assistant bards do well not to speak until spoken to, all the ladies together cannot help being flattered by the attentions of six fine, young, eligible bachelors like Lord Ysgard's sons. I believe their parents are—er—willing to consider suitable offers."

"Willing?" Torchyld snorted. "Aunt Edelgysa practically—"

"So she did, now that you mention it. Mothers always like to make sure their daughters have ample dowries, don't they? Been filling hope chests ever since the girls lisped their first infant words, I don't doubt. And with King Sfyn's—er—famed munificence, I'm sure the arrangements would be satisfactory to all parties, should these lads succeed in winning the hands of the young ladies. Is there a barber in the castle?"

"A barber?" faltered Lord Ysgard. "Degwel, do we have a barber?"

"We had one, but it was stolen by King Sfyn's men when they abducted our kitchen maids," Degwel replied with great presence of mind.

"Oh yes, so it was. We've been meaning to buy a new one, but ye know how it is. Er—what did ye want ye barber for, noble bard?"

"I just thought we might tidy the boys up a bit. Trim their hair, wash their necks, make them more presentable. After all, princesses are bound to have a good many gentlemen callers. Competition's pretty fierce over at King Sfyn's, I understand. Princes and lords and knights errant and traveling salesmen lined up in rows, all clamoring for the hand of Gwendolyn or Guinevere or one of the other girls."

"I marvel these fair princesses be not yet espoused, with suitors so thick on ye ground," Degwel observed with the merest hint of a sneer.

"M'yes. Well, you know how young ladies are." Peter sang a few bars of "Some Day My Prince Will Come" to illustrate his point. "The problem is, they may all be getting fed up with waiting for the right prince to come along. I'd say you lads ought not to lose any time getting started. How far is it to Sfynfford, anyway? I shouldn't think it's any great distance if they're always popping over here on wench-napping expeditions."

"It be a vast distance," said Yfor. "A half day's march afoot, at least. Less by horse, in sooth."

"Ten miles or so, I expect," Shandy remarked to Stott.

Dan nodded his head profoundly. He was pleasantly stuffed with eels and inclined to somnolence, but he roused himself enough to say, "You spoke of barbering. I may be permitted without undue accusation of immodesty to remind you that in my hot-blooded youth I once held the national slow-clip sheep shearing championship."

"So you did, by George. Then a spot of haircutting ought to be right up your alley, if we can find you anything to cut with. A sharp knife would do, I expect. Anything you could do to change those kids' looks would have to be an improvement. Nice if we could clean them up a little. I wonder if it's possible to manufacture soft soap out of wood ashes and eel fat?"

"I can manage that, I think," said Tim. "Hilda Horsefall was telling me once how they used to do it back before the soap works was started over at Lumpkin Corners. They used tallow, not eel fat, but what the hell?"

"Then let's get cracking."

Ysgard's sons were just the excuse they needed to hotfoot it for Sfynfford, but if they were going to peddle the boys as prospective bridegrooms, they'd have to improve the product. Shandy rounded up some knives and set Dan and Torchyld to sharpening them, while he helped Timothy Ames start their own soap factory.

Tim's kettle attracted a good deal of attention for the rest of that day, though surreptitious tasters were somewhat disappointed in the flavor of his brew. When he at last managed to produce a curdy mess that actually worked up a lather and removed dirt, though, all hands were vastly impressed.

To be sure, the natives couldn't figure out quite *why* the archdruid should be interested in removing those layers of grime Lord Ysgard's sons had been so patiently collecting all their lives. They decided it must be some esoteric rite of passage. Anyway, it was interesting to watch the youths turn color in the tub.

Once they were bathed, Dan Stott produced a short knife he'd borrowed from Lord Ysgard and honed to razor sharpness. He had to demonstrate his intentions on Tim's beard before the young men would let him touch them. Once they'd grasped the idea, though, they were charmed at the novelty and willingly submitted to being barbered. Cleaned up and dressed in freshly laundered tunics, they turned out to be a far more well-favored lot than first impressions had led Shandy to expect.

Lord Ysgard was unreasonably proud of himself, as fathers are apt to be, for having sired such a personable collection of sons, though none too happy when it came time to open his strong room and fetch forth six engagement presents rich enough to tempt a king's granddaughters. He kept on grumbling about the high cost of wooing until Peter Shandy, who'd strolled out beside the moat to watch the eels swim by, happened to spy Medrus draw his lordship aside and whisper something in his ear.

Whatever he said perked Lord Ysgard up amazingly. Peter could see the lord questioning the ex-clerk eagerly, nodding and sticking out his under lip, waving his hands and all but licking his chops. Then Medrus said something else and Ysgard's eyebrows shot up. This was as good as a play. Ysgard was trying to say no. Medrus was giving him a sales talk. Ysgard was falling for it. He was beginning to look furtive. Medrus was looking furtiver. Shandy recalled the impulse he'd had back in the coracle to kick Medrus overboard and wondered why he hadn't yielded to it. What was the little sneak up to now?

He wished there were some way he could get close enough to overhear what they were talking about, but cover was sparse around the moat. So was Medrus's beard, and that would have made lip reading fairly feasible if he'd been obliging enough to keep his face turned toward Shandy. Instead, he kept his mouth close to Ysgard's ear, which was now cocked even more sharply than before although its owner's face was still registering conflicting emotions. Shandy could make out one word, though, because Medrus kept saying it over and over. He could swear it was "Dwydd."

CHAPTER 10

That miserable son of a bitch! Whatever Medrus was selling Lord Ysgard a bill of goods about couldn't be anything savory if King Sfyn's resident hag was mixed up in it. Peter watched the pair separate and sneak into the castle by different doors. Then he came out from behind the bush he'd been using for cover and went inside, too.

It must be time to eat again; he could smell boiled eels. They reminded him of an old ballad: What got ye from your sweetheart, Randall my son? And Randall said eels and eel broth. And then Randall's mother made his bed and he lay down on it and died from the eels his sweetheart had poisoned. Shandy decided he'd better not eat any eels tonight. Tim hadn't better, either, nor Dan, nor most particularly Torchyld. Where was he?

He asked a passing vassal. "Have you seen my apprentice? It's time for his music lesson."

"He sleepeth, sire," was the reply.

"Where?"

"On ye battlements, sire."

"Show me."

"Sire, my master hath sent me to dish up ye eels."

"They can wait. Show me. Quick."

The serf didn't like this but, being a serf, he didn't dare disobey. He led the way up an unbelievably narrow, twisty stone staircase to what Peter Shandy in his ignorance would have called the roof. There, dreaming perhaps of his troth-plighting days, lay Torchyld, his golden hair glinting in the sun and his bardic robe rucked up around his thighs. He was a magnificent specimen of young gianthood, no doubt about that. And he was still breathing. Just to make sure, Peter reached out to take his pulse. His hand stopped in mid-reach.

On the battlements stood a row of boulders, ready to be cast down, Shandy supposed, on the heads of enemies. Up through the crenellations in the wall grew a vine: a sturdy, thrifty creeper that looked picturesque as all get-out but was no sort of thing for a prudent castellan to have growing where some marauder could climb up it, or a man-at-arms get his foot caught in it. Lord Ysgard ought to know better, Shandy was thinking, when he noticed a loop of the vine had been artfully led around the biggest of the boulders, then twined around Torchyld's left ankle. If the young knight were to leap up suddenly, he'd dislodge the boulder, get dragged over the parapet, and crack his skull on the stones below. And people would say, "Such a promising young knight. What a pity he couldn't have looked where he put his feet."

Moving with utmost care, Peter lifted the loop away from the boulder. He was untangling Torchyld's feet when, as he'd anticipated, the king's great-nephew woke, tried to get up, and was brought low.

"What hit me?" he roared.

"You've been the intended victim of another assassination plot," Shandy told him. "Lie still while I get you untangled."

"Ungh? What mean ye? What plot, forsooth?"

Peter explained the simple but potentially lethal mechanism. "As I expect you realize by now," he finished, "somebody's extremely anxious to have you dead."

"Owain," said Torchyld promptly. "He craves to wed my Syglinde. Fain be I to tear out his eyeballs and shove them up his—"

"Owain isn't here."

"He sent somebody."

"Who?"

In fact, Peter Shandy was fairly certain he knew who. That tableau he'd witnessed down by the moat would fit in tidily here. Medrus could have arranged the trap, then gone to convince Lord Ysgard it was a good idea.

But why? Had Gwrach and Dwydd been cooking up some

deal in which Torchyld's death would have been more than just another free lunch for the sorceress? Mooching around the cave between guide jobs, Medrus must have had plenty of opportunities to poke his glow into Gwrach's doings. Did he know what the hags were up to, and had he decided to carry the plot through, counting on Dwydd to reward him later, either voluntarily or through a spot of blackmail?

Peter thought he'd better not mention any of this to Torchyld until he was sure of his facts. There must surely be a great deal of resentment among all the men in Ysgard about their kidnapped women. The Sfynfford men couldn't have begun the mass abductions until after Torchyld had killed the wyvern, since there would have been little point in carrying off a girl one day only to have her eaten the next.

Torchyld himself claimed the deed had made him famous. No doubt all that nudging and whispering in the banqueting hall meant Lord Ysgard's sons and the other men had guessed quickly enough who this enchanted apprentice from the court of King Sfyn really was. Maybe the would-be murderer was just some lovesick swain seeking revenge for the loss of his girl friend.

In any event, Peter decided, it would be best not to voice any suspicions until he was sure of his ground. Torchyld was an impulsive chap, and Lord Ysgard's castle was a dismal enough place without bits of Medrus strewn in the corners.

Right now, Torchyld was irate enough. "How should I know whom Owain sent?" he snarled.

"Would you recognize one of the servants from your great-uncle's castle?"

"Aye, verily."

"You haven't seen any of them around here, have you?"

"They could be under enchantment."

"And I could be your grandmother," Peter snorted. "Forget about enchantments, can't you?"

"Nay. I be under one."

"The hell you be."

"Ye mean ye hast disenchanted me? O great druid!"

Shandy all but got his ribs fractured by Torchyld's embrace.

"All right," he wheezed, "you're disenchanted. Feel any different?"

"I feel—" Torchyld had to stop and think it over. "Nay, I wot not how I feel."

"M'well, that's normal. You'll get sorted out sooner or later I expect. How do Owain and Dwydd get along?"

"Owain getteth along with nobody for long. Nor doth Dwydd, save for her own fell purposes."

"And what would those purposes be?"

"She craveth to rule."

"You mean she's after King Sfyn's job?"

"Nay, she would have control over ye king and all his court. And ye birds that fly over ye battlements and ye mice that nibble ye crumbs from ye banqueting table, and e'en ye spiders in ye dungeon. It seemeth me she may have ye spiders under her vile thumb already. There be some woundily mean spiders back at ye castle."

"I'm not sure spiders are germane to the issue," said Peter. "Aside from Dwydd's lust for power and Owain's lust for Syglinde, what reason might any member of King Sfyn's court have for wanting you dead? Have you made enemies?"

"Who, me? How could I, being so lovable?"

"But you said the lot of them were ready enough to pin the rap on you for having kidnapped your great-uncle's griffin. You claimed they're all jealous because you were the one who killed the wyvern."

"Oh, that. Eftsoons they will repent."

"Think so? They weren't exactly struggling to save your bacon when they saw you thrust forth into the wilderness with no weapon but a harp. They must have known you were no better qualified to be a bard than I am to be a lady in waiting. None of them ran after you with a box lunch or a clean pair of socks, did they? And what about when you went to hunt the wyvern? Couldn't somebody have lent you a decent sword?"

"Nobody happed to have one handy," Torchyld muttered.

"Couldn't somebody have gone and got one?"

"It be against ye rules."

"Who makes the rules?"

"I wot not. Anybody who happeth to think of one, me-seems."

"Then why couldn't somebody make a new rule that it was illegal to face a wyvern with a disenchanted sword, or something?"

"They wist not ye sword was dulled."

"I see. How many of your relatives were around at the time?"

"All of them. They always are. That be why Syglinde and I crave our own castle."

"Which you intend to pay for with the wyvern's hoard, right?"

"True, O tedious druid."

"How much of the hoard do you expect to have left over when the castle's finished?"

"Great abundance. Vast be ye hoard."

"Where is it now?"

"My great-uncle had it transported from ye wyvern's lair to ye castle's strong room."

"How do you know it's not—er—getting mixed up with the king's own treasure?"

"Because Great-uncle Sfyn keepeth his shut up in stout oaken chests. Mine be open to sight on ye floor. There were not enough chests in ye kingdom to hold it," Torchyld said smugly.

"Um. Who keeps the key to the strong room?"

"Great-uncle Sfyn, in sooth."

"And what if anything should—er—happen to your great-uncle?"

"Then Uncle Edmyr would be crowned king and get to keep ye key."

"But he can't get hold of it now?"

"Nay, none toucheth it save ye king. That be ye rule."

"How did you get your treasure into the strong room, then?"

"Great-uncle Sfyn oped ye door for me. Dwydd had to un-spell ye room so I could go in. And Syggie, too. She wanted to share in ye geste. So did mine uncles and cousins and aunts, but I made Dwydd say them nay."

"That's interesting," said Peter. "Which of your uncles gets along best with Dwydd?"

"She sucketh up to Uncle Edmyr, he being crown prince, but he liketh her not."

"Then you don't think he'd keep her on as—er—resident hag if he were to become king?"

"Nay, he would. Ye new king sacketh not an old retainer e'en gin he hateth her guts. It be not ye done thing."

"I see. Getting back to your own hoard, who would inherit if anything happened to you?"

"Syglinde would, gin we were wed. But we be not. And now—"

"Stop it," barked Shandy. "Blubbering won't help. I told you we were going back. We'll find her, never fear."

"When do we leave?"

"The sooner the better. Lord Ysgard's sons can guide us. I only hope your cousin Guinevere and the rest haven't all gone and got themselves engaged before we arrive."

"No fear," Torchyld assured him. "Aunt Aldora, Aunt Edelgysa, and Aunt Gwynedd have been trying to palm them off on every halfway eligible lord who cometh along, but they haven't managed yet."

"How do the young ladies themselves feel about matrimony?"

"They be all so sick of their mothers' nagging, they be ready to go and get themselves carried off by a swarm of dragons so some luckless gull of a knight will come along and rescue them. Then he would have to wed them."

"All of them?"

"Nay, I meant one dragon and one knight apiece. That be ye done thing."

"I see. Then your aunts and your cousins as well would be glad to see Lord Ysgard's sons."

"Aye, verily. Ye young lords be no great catches, but they be none so bad-looking wights, and they comen out of ye right drawer. 'Tis pity Castle Ysgard be so small, but perchance they can build on a wing or two."

"I suspect Lord Ysgard may have something of the sort in mind," Shandy observed. "I have a hunch he and Medrus are launching a fund-raising drive."

"Going back for Gwrach's hoard," Torchyld grunted. "Why ye hell not? Lord Ysgard will have need of it gin he getteth my cousins for daughters-in-law."

"No doubt. How did you know that's what they've been cooking up?"

"Forsooth, be I a cabbage-head? Somebody might as well. We need it not. Ye sons should go instead of their father, but I be not ye one to tell them so. What if Gwrach hath a sister? There be but one suitor apiece for my cousins so it behooveth me not to let one get slain. Gin I show up a bridegroom short, all hell will be to pay. With a full company, I may have time to get my armor on before they notice I ha' not also brought Ffyff. Ah, what a relief to be disenchanted!"

"Why?" Peter asked him. "In what way are you different now from what you were a little while ago?"

"Dumb question, ecod! I be me again, Torchyld ye Valiant, betrothed of Syglinde ye Beautiful."

"You don't look any different. Cleaner, I'll grant you, but that's on account of the archdruid's soap." Torchyld, ever alert for new deeds of derring-do, had insisted on being first to try the squashy result of Tim's experiment.

"The point I'm trying to make, Torchyld, is that you allowed yourself to believe you'd been enchanted just because Dwydd handed you a harp and made you change your clothes. You're now under the delusion I've disenchanted you just because I've made some remark to that effect; but the fact is, you've never been anybody but Torchyld the Valiant all along. Dwydd may have a knack for growing hogweed, but in my considered opinion, her so-called enchantments are nothing but stage magic."

"But my sword?"

"When you get back to your great-uncle's castle, take a good look around. I'll bet you dollars to doughnuts you'll find a rock somewhere handy that's got some fresh scars on it from having been bashed repeatedly with a sharp metal object.''

"What? Why, that old—"

"Precisely. As to Lady Syglinde and the griffin, I further suspect Dwydd worked their disappearance by throwing something on the fire that temporarily blinded everybody else in the banqueting hall so that she, and possibly some co-conspirator, could hustle them out of sight.''

"She hath not disembodied them, as Gwrach did Medrus?"

"M'well, it's a possibility, I suppose, but I'm skeptical. Have you ever known her to disembody anyone before?"

"Nay," Torchyld admitted.

"We have a saying in my country that goes, I'll believe it when I see it. My own father used to add, you'd better make sure you know what you're seeing before you start believing. You see, Torchyld, people like to believe in magic. The idea that it's some human or quasi-human person who's making strange things happen is less awesome than the real miracles, such as ourselves and the world around us, that we can't explain at all. This makes it easier for the Dwydds and Gwraches to get away with tricks that support the notion they have powers they may not in fact possess. The more we believe in their powers, the less apt we are to notice we're being fooled. Once we realize it is in fact all foolishness and learn to laugh at it, their so-called enchantments blow up in their faces.''

"Gwrach blew up in ours."

"My point exactly. She couldn't endure being laughed at. Those who set themselves up as being greater than the rest of us never can. Remember that.''

"But what if they really be greater than ye rest?"

"Then they'd be laughing, too. That's how you tell.''

"Great be thy wisdom, druid. Or bard, or whatever ye be.''

"I think I'd like to go on being a bard for a while. You haven't heard me recite 'Casey at the Bat' yet.''

"Verily, ye be unlike any bard I ever ran across.''

"No doubt," said Peter rather complacently. "Come on, then, let's go nuzzle up to the trough. I'd suggest, however, that you lay off the boiled eels tonight.''

"But why, forsooth? I like boiled eels. And boiled eels like me."

"These particular eels may not. Remember what I was just telling you about magic tricks? I have a hunch Medrus and Lord Ysgard may be trying a few, with the object of keeping you from ever getting back to Sfynfford."

"For what reason, prithee?"

"Because Dwydd wants you dead and Medrus may know why. Don't you see it yet? That business of ruining your sword before you faced the wyvern, and then sending the hogweed to chase you into Gwrach's clutches were just fancied-up attempts to murder you."

"Then why did she not just kill me back at ye castle?"

"Probably because King Sfyn might have taken umbrage in a rather large way if she did. How do you get along with your great-uncle, by and large?"

"He thinketh I be ye wyvern's whiskers. Or did, until Dwydd cooked up yon lie about me poofing old Ffyff."

"There you are. You see, she's undermining your position at court so that if she succeeds in getting you killed, she won't get the punishment she deserves. Except of course that we're not going to let her succeed, and we're going to let King Sfyn know what she's been up to."

"He will believe you not."

"He'll believe me, never you fear. But anyway, that's why it's important for you to get not only the bridegrooms but also yourself back there safe and sound. So lay off the boiled eels. Also the drinking horn."

"Then what be I to eat?"

"Only what I myself give you."

"And why should I trust you?"

"Good question. You're already profiting by my little speech, I see. Very well, then, if you're nervous about relying on me, maybe you'd rather go out and hunt yourself a rabbit or something. Either that or go hungry. That wouldn't kill you for one meal, surely."

"It would do me no good," Torchyld snarled, "gin we be

heading for home betimes. A soldier needeth something to march on besides his feet."

"Then use your head. Don't take anything that would be easy to put poison into. That's why I told you to leave the drinking horn alone. The person next to you could slip in a pinch of something deadly, knowing you pride yourself on draining the horn to the tip, so he wouldn't be likely to kill anybody else. It would also be easy to poison one eel in the trencher—the biggest I'd say, because that's the one you always grab unless somebody else beats you to it. But it would be hard to poison venison because the minions always bring on a whole haunch and the poisoner would have no way of knowing where you'd take a cut from. Do you see what I'm driving at?"

"I do. Well spoken, bard. Let us forthwith to ye banqueting hall. We must also guard lest ye archdruid or ye assistant archdruid eat poison meant for me. Or ye six young lords. Let my cousins poison them once they be wed, gin they wist. Right now, I need them alive."

CHAPTER 11

No, Shandy thought a little while later, you couldn't call young Torchyld slow on the uptake. He'd already upset a trencherful of boiled eels all over Degwel's paunch. Now he was pressing Lord Ysgard to take the first quaff from the newly filled drinking horn that had just been passed to him. Lord Ysgard was refusing.

"Not at ye moment, thank you. I have matters of grave import to discuss with my sons. Drink up, assistant bard of noble birth."

He turned to his offspring. "Sons, I'm afraid ye must postpone your visit to King Sfyn. I need ye here to guard the castle. I have to tootle off on a secret mission."

"What secret mission?" demanded his son Yfor.

"If I went around telling everybody, it wouldn't be much of a secret, would it?"

"Blah," said Yfor. "I be not going to sit around here cooling my heels, forsooth, for any secret mission. Ye but wist to hightail it over to King Sfyn's castle before us and select ye fairest and fattest virgin for thyself, ye unpaternal old goat. Ye can stay here and guard thine own castle. I be not having you spoil my chances with Princess Imogene. Or was it Princess Gwendolyn?"

"I want Gwendolyn," yelled Yorich.

"How do ye know?" said Torchyld. "Ye ha' not seen her yet."

"I like ye name. Gwendolyn," Yorich murmured dreamily, wiping venison grease off his chin with the back of his hand. "It soundeth like ye slow dripping of roasting eel fat into ye coals on a blustery winter night when ye hounds lie content around ye fire and a man dreameth of sharing his sheepskins with a fair and willing damsel. Be she lovely beyond compare, assistant bard?"

"She be willing," Torchyld answered cautiously, "and she hath abundance of prime quality sheepskins. Ye could be comfortable with Gwendolyn, Yorich."

"Not more comfortable than I with Princess Imogene," cried Yfor.

"Nay, not more," Torchyld assured him. "Imogene be fatter."

"And she hath also good store of sheepskins?"

"In sooth. They all do. And fine gowns and rich embroideries and gewgaws and folderols. And they can dance right featly and make possets and sweetmeats and—"

"Take baths?" shouted Huw.

"Aye, verily. They take baths all ye time," said their cousin grandly.

"With soap?"

"Think ye King Sfyn would stint his granddaughters on anything that pertaineth to their rank and dignity?"

"At least now we know what to give them for a wedding present," Timothy Ames whispered to Peter.

Lord Ysgard's sons were by now all a-clamor. "Father, how can ye even think of asking us to put off our wooing? E'en now, trains of noble suitors may be wending their way to ye palace of King Sfyn, lured by ye far-flung fame of ye fair-featured females."

"I'faith, noble apprentice bard," Medrus insinuated, "gin they be so fair, I marvel these princesses ye tell of be not all wed long ago."

"They be maids of tender years," Torchyld roared. "Dost give me ye lie, cave-crawler?"

"Of course he doesn't," said Peter. "Sit down, Torchyld."

Peter wasn't about to let his assistant get into any kind of brawl, in the course of which somebody could slip a poisoned dagger between his ribs. He suspected Degwel, the smarmy steward, could produce one if asked. He'd further venture to opine that Degwel wouldn't take much coaxing. It was plain the steward didn't care much for what was happening around here.

Understandably enough, Peter supposed. With no women around to interfere, Degwel had been running things to suit himself. Now here he was, faced with the prospect of six new mistresses in one lump. It was hardly to be supposed the steward wouldn't be anxious about how he might keep hold of the reins, and quite possibly he'd decide he'd better do more than sit and worry. The sooner they cleared out of here, the better.

There was to be no wassailing around the banqueting board tonight, that was clear. Lord Ysgard was champing at the bit to get away, and Medrus was egging him on.

"I want no more argy-bargy," Ysgard was roaring at his sons. "Ye can go and get ye princesses when I have performed my geste."

"That be no fair," shouted Yfan. "Ye already had a geste, when ye rode forth and rescued Mama from ye wandering minstrel."

"Call that a geste? I had to rescue her six more times before I finally said ye hell with it and let her go. Be warned by your father, lads, never rescue a maiden until ye be sure she craveth to be rescued. Not that ye ever pay any attention to anything I say. It be not like ye good old days, when sons had some filial respect for their fathers. Now when I attempt some sage precept, ye just tell me to blow it out my ear and go on your merry way. Ye'll go hotfooting after those princesses thinking they be going to have ye heralds out on ye drawbridge to welcome ye with fanfare of trumpets. And what will ye get? Like as not, they'll just tell ye to buzz off because they be all in love with ye stable boy. Pour boiling oil down your necks, I shouldn't be surprised."

"They will not," snarled Torchyld. "Ye granddaughters of King Sfyn be models of deportment and good breeding. They say so themselves."

"There, see," said Hayward.

"Save it, Hay," said his eldest brother. "Fare forth fearlessly,

Father. We shall man ye battlements as ye command, and make plans for our own expedition whilst watching ye safely away."

"Good boy," said Lord Ysgard. "Well, come on, Medrus. We can't lollygag around here all night. Be ye boat ready?"

"It be provisioned and waiting, Grandiosity. Thanks to ye good offices of thy faithful steward Degwel," Medrus added diplomatically. Despite his humble beginnings, he appeared to have the makings of a courtier.

"Then we wayfarers will wish you a happy and successful— er—geste," said Peter Shandy, "and thank you for your hospitality."

"Ye pleasure will, I hope, have been mostly mine," Lord Ysgard rejoined with a meaning look at Medrus.

Thus with fair words and much display of courtesy, the parties separated: most of them to the battlements; Medrus and Lord Ysgard, looking sickeningly pleased with themselves, to the jetty. Daniel Stott shook his majestic head as he watched them embark in the little boat that had brought him and his companions to the castle.

"I hope Medrus has inside information as to whether that coracle is indeed a regular ferry between this castle and the vicinage of Gwrach's cave. To the best of my recollection, such assumptions are not always safe to be taken for granted."

"All the more reason, then, why we be loath to dally here waiting for them to come back afore we embark on our own geste," said Yfor.

"But you promised to stay and man ye battlements," Huw objected.

"I said we'd man ye battlements to watch him safely away. I made no promises about afterward. Once ye boat gets around yon bend, we march. Right, brothers?"

"Right," they howled. "Strike up a brave marching song, O bard."

"Not so hasty," said Peter. "First, how many of us are going on this expedition?"

"I be," said Torchyld.

Shandy damned well was, and so were Stott and Ames, or he'd know the reason why. None of the six brothers would be left behind. That left Degwel and the men-at-arms, along with the scullions, minions, and whatever other lower orders there might be, to defend the castle. Degwel expressed himself as being perfectly fit for the job. Shandy decided he probably was, since it wouldn't be for long anyway.

Lord Yfor, as regent in his father's absence, summoned the castle's entire complement to a conference in the great hall. Boiled eels were served and flagons of ale passed around; then he delivered his oration.

"Men of Ysgard! As ye know, my father hath embarked on a geste we know not whither with ye clerk Medrus. Little do we wot how long he may be away, or in what state he may return. We wish him good fortune on his parlous journey, but in his absence, we must think of ourselves. This sudden turn of events putteth us even more at risk than our womanless condition hath heretofore left us.

"Bethink yourselves! For lo, these many moons there hath been no patter of little feet within our walls, save when a cook beheadeth a fowl. All solace, all softening female influence, all mending of tunics and combing of nits hath been denied to us. For ye welfare of us all and ye survival of Ysgard, therefore, my brothers and I have sworn a mighty oath. We propose to make ye journey so many of our maidens have already accomplished: namely and to wit, to Sfynfford."

"Do not leave us," came the frantic cries.

"Nay, list," shouted Yfor. "We do not stay. We but woo and win ye six fair granddaughters of King Sfyn and bring them back here, along with their chambermaids and serving wenches, all of whom be plump and comely, according to last recorded estimate."

Torchyld nodded enthusiastically. "And unattached, and eager to meet a bunch of strapping men-at-arms and lusty minions of all types. And they all hath sisters, too, ecod. In sooth, owing to ye recent influx from Ysgard, King Sfyn be somewhat overstocked with nubile maidens at ye moment. At Sfynfford be wives enough for all."

"Then on to Ysgard," shouted the corporal of the guard.

The cry was taken up and the situation threatened to get out of hand, until Daniel Stott arose, laid down the eel he'd been eating, and surveyed the company with that air of benign but implacable calm he used on Bashan of Balaclava when the college's prize bull was feeling rambunctious.

"The union of man and woman in lawful wedlock," he reminded them when the racket had subsided, "is not a matter to be undertaken in a spirit of ribaldry and untrammeled lust."

There was one shout of, "Huzzah for untrammeled lust," but it was quickly suppressed. Stott continued.

"The march to Sfynfford will be carried out in a spirit of due solemnity and knightly courtesy. The participants will be Lord Yfor and his five brothers, Sir Torchyld, Archdruid Ames, myself, and Bard Shandy. It will be your privilege to remain on guard here under the direction of your officers and your able steward Degwel."

He exchanged a courteous nod with that other grave and portly dignitary. "Guided by the honorable Degwel, you must proceed forthwith to cleanse the castle and prepare it by every means in your power for the reception of the six princesses and their attendant ladies. It may be here stated that before we leave, the archdruid will entrust to the honorable Degwel his secret formula for making soap."

Murmurs of awe and reverence spread through the assemblage. Degwel swelled even larger than usual with this new augmentation of his importance. "There will be soap for those who merit ye largesse," he announced with lofty benignity.

"You will manage everything with wisdom and justice, I'm sure," said Shandy. "Er—you needn't worry about the contents of the strong room. The archdruid has put a strong spell on the lock, so that a fearsome fate will overtake any miscreant who gets any funny ideas about Lord Ysgard's treasure."

"Oh?" Degwel's composure wobbled slightly. "Wouldst care to describe ye spell, noble bard?"

"It's rather a speciality of the archdruid's, actually. You might well call it a fate worse than death, because it first makes the would-be thief a laughingstock among all people, then reduces him to the state of the lowliest thing that crawls. Naturally it can't affect anybody who's honest and true to his trust, so you, noble Degwel, have nothing to fear. Nor does anybody else who performs his duty faithfully during the very short time Lord Yfor and his brothers will be away."

"Ye return not with ye young lords?"

"Perhaps. Perhaps not. No doubt you'll be receiving an honor guard and a deputation from King Sfyn, however. They may come on ahead, so don't shoot at any soldiers until you've made sure they're not your future in-laws."

Amid cheers and laughter, the wooing party set off. The younger brothers had been loud in their demands to go in style, on horseback, but the elder ones had scruples against depriving the men-at-arms of six good mounts during Lord Ysgard's absence. Torchyld assured them that was quite all right; the princesses would be quite willing to love them for themselves alone, so long as they brought nice presents. Since Lord Ysgard had already selected a choice assortment, that was no problem. They just bundled the baubles into their pouches and beelined it for Sfynfford.

The going wasn't bad, even by moonlight. There'd been so much traffic of late, between the abductors and the would-be abductees, that the path was well worn. Seeing this, the six brothers set such a pace that Peter again grew anxious for Tim, and insisted they construct a litter to carry him. Tim protested, but Peter shushed him.

"For Christ's sake, Tim, remember your dignity. You're supposed to be head man in charge here. If you arrive at King Sfyn's court out of wind and reeking like a horse, you'll ruin the show before we get a chance to do our stuff."

"What in hell are we supposed to do, anyway?"

"Search me. We'll know when we get there. We haven't managed too badly so far, have we?"

"We've got rid of that smarmy little son of a bitch Medrus, anyway."

"M'yes, and I have a hunch we ought to be glad we did. I just hope Lord Ysgard won't find out he's bitten off more than he can chew."

"Serve him right, the ornery sidewinder. Though I suppose

I shouldn't run him down. He was generous enough with his eel grease."

"By the way, did you in fact remember to give Degwel the recipe?"

"Sure, why not? I wasn't about to spend the rest of my life, assuming I have any left, stirring a stinking soap kettle. Pete, do you honestly think we'll ever get out of this crazy mess?"

"Ask Dan. He's the expert on never-never land."

"He's contemplating his—Jesus, what's that?"

A hideous growling, whirfling howl was rending the air and cracking the treetops. The six brothers were clutching each other in panic. Daniel Stott had assumed a posture of grave concern. Only Torchyld showed no fear, but charged headlong toward the frightful sound.

"For God's sake, Torchyld, come back!"

Without reflecting that he must be losing his own mind to act so, Peter charged after his apprentice, yelling and waving the three useless wands he was still, for some reason, lugging around. His example emboldened the rest to run after them, all except Daniel Stott, who merely briskened his walk. Thus it was the whole brigade that burst into the clearing whence came the direful roaring.

And there beheld the awestruck group a sight to make the hottest blood run cold. A great, winged creature with the body of a lion and the wings of an eagle was rearing up on its gruesome talons to strike. And Torchyld was laughing his head off!

"He runneth mad," cried Hywell.

"To ye rescue!" cried Hayward.

"Now Hay runneth mad," cried Yfan, tripping up his youngest sibling and sitting down on him for his own good.

"What be we to do?" cried Yfor. "We be not cravens to just stand here and watch—arrgh!"

The monster was opening its vast mouth, sticking out its huge tongue, lunging its head at Torchyld. He, seeming unmindful of this dire peril, merely ducked, laughed harder, and punched at the huge beast's chest with his bare fist.

Then Torchyld was down on the ground, wrestling with the

monster. Then the monster was on its back, waggling its talons in the air, for all the world like a foolish puppy. And Torchyld was up on his knees beside it, rubbing its belly!

"Aw, ye silly old griffin. What ye hell hast been up to, scaring us all into fits and making Great-uncle Sfyn feel bad? Come, puff a little fire for His Majesty."

The griffin puffed, but achieved only a lopsided smoke ring.

"Hey, Ffyff, art feeling off thy feed? What hath that old bat been a-doing to ye?"

"May I be of service?" Daniel Stott had intrepidly advanced to Torchyld's side. "Am I to infer this is not a well griffin?"

"Nay, I know not. Ffyff hath always breathed fire before." Torchyld was running his hands over the vast body, feeling for signs of injury. "He feeleth not—I wot not how to say it."

"Allow me."

Stott knelt beside the griffin. The six sons of Lord Ysgard sucked in their breath. Tim muttered, "Cripes." Peter said nothing. Dan knew his stuff. He rubbed and pressed, felt the griffin's beak, put his ear to the heaving chest and listened to its heartbeat.

"I did him no hurt?" Torchyld was asking anxiously. "I meant not to be rough. 'Twas but that I was o'erjoyed to see him."

"He was equally gratified to see you, I am sure," Stott replied. "I suspect his affliction to be mostly fatigue and perhaps malnourishment. He is, as you have explained, an elderly griffin, and one used to what might be termed the easy life, though no doubt performing his court duties with punctilio. I should venture to suggest this griffin may have been held captive in too confined a space and deprived of adequate rations, possibly with the idea of weakening him and thus making him more amenable to captivity. Fortunately he cannot have been imprisoned long enough to effect serious debility. Against this factor, however, must be weighed his advanced age. I can find no serious injury, but there is a definite tremor in the wing joints and a general flaccidity in the muscles, along with shortness of breath and a rapid heartbeat that would be consistent with exhaustion. The noble beast has obviously managed to escape his prison and fly some distance."

"To meet me! Good old Ffyff. But what be we to do?"

"I should say our wisest move at this juncture will be to camp here with him for the night, feeding him at intervals from the stock of cold boiled eels I brought as provision for the march, and keeping him well watered. I mention boiled eels, Sir Torchyld—that is to say, apprentice bard—because you say he is accustomed to such food as you yourself eat. Perhaps you might select a succulent tidbit and try him with it."

"Ye be going to feed that griffin our food?" demanded Yfan. He was, as Peter had noted earlier, inclined to be greedy.

"I am going to feed him my own food," Stott replied with vast dignity. "For a beast of his size, adequate nutritional intake is essential to the maintenance of full vigor. His need, as Sir Philip Sidney will one day put it, is greater than mine. Perhaps you would be good enough to fetch water from yonder spring I hear trickling, so we can give him a drink. According to the literature, your helmet would make a suitable receptacle."

Chastened, Yfan went to get the water.

CHAPTER 12

Peter offered to take a turn sitting up with the griffin, but Dan and Torchyld wouldn't hear of it. Dan was quite happy having a large animal to doctor, even when its affliction involved its inability to breathe fire; a circumstance for which the cows, sheep, pigs, and horses of Balaclava Agricultural College had not prepared him.

Torchyld was even happier merely to sit beside the griffin with that immense beaked head resting against his knee, stroking the long wing feathers and bursting forth with an occasional, "Aw, ye fat old griffin, ye," at which Ffyffnyr would beat his long, skinny tail with its arrow-pointed tip against the ground and purr for a while before falling into another griffin-sized catnap.

As dawn broke, Dan Stott found a patch of catnip growing beside the stream from which they'd been baling Ffyffnyr's drinking water. From this, he managed to concoct a medication which so improved the griffin's condition that he coughed up enough sparks to light a small cooking fire. This enabled Stott to brew several quarts of catnip tea, using the young lords' helmets for cooking pots. So efficacious was this potion that after a few helmetfuls, Ffyffnyr belched a wonderful globe of blue-green fire with vermilion trimmings and was pronounced ready to travel.

The six prematurely lovesick swains all had some catnip tea, too. They'd grumbled at the enforced rest, being of a mind to march by night and burst upon their unwitting ladies by sunrise. Shandy, however, had managed to convince them that they must give the princessess time for their morning baths before arriving.

Anyway, they had to wait for Torchyld and the griffin. If

they'd gone barging up to the castle without proper introductions, they'd have been more apt to get a hail of spears through their gizzards than tender maidens' greetings.

The catnip tea and a snack of bread and meat spared from Ffyffnyr's breakfast perked them up. Then Shandy led the six embryo fiancés down to where the spring widened out into a pool, and made them take morning baths. When they got back to the campsite, they found Dan and Torchyld still bending over Ffyffnyr.

In the daylight, the griffin was even more awesome than he'd appeared at their moonlight meeting. The rich scarlet of his coat, like no other fur they could ever have imagined, shimmered as the morning sun struck it. The feathers on his wings and legs were that intense red of a scarlet tanager's, almost incandescent in the brilliance of their coloring. Shandy noticed, however, that both fur and feathers were rubbed and frayed in spots. One great flight feather was broken, its tip flapping loose, and Stott was gravely debating whether to amputate.

Peter went over to examine the damage at close range, too. "That's funny," he was beginning to say, when Torchyld interrupted him.

"Look!"

"At his collar, you mean?"

"This be no collar. 'Tis a braid of my darling Syglinde's hair."

Sure enough, Peter was looking at an elaborately plaited strand the color of spun gold, cunningly intertwined to fit snugly and securely around the griffin's neck.

"By George, so it is. What a marvelous color. I gather Ffyffnyr wasn't wearing this when you saw him last?"

"Nay. I told ye he'd but a collar of gold set with gems. Naught so fine as this."

"The gold collar wasn't—er—welded on or anything? Lady Syglinde could have got it off without too much trouble?"

"She must have." Torchyld was caressing the plait with his fingertips. "This be a pattern none save my Syglinde can braid. She made me a baldric for my sword in this same wise, from strips of colored leather. 'Twas not done in a moment, I can tell ye.''

"M'yes," said Peter. "I'm no pigtail expert myself, but I can see this is a beautiful job of braiding. I'd say she must have done it yesterday after she and the griffin were both spirited away. That means they were put in the same hiding place together. Would Lady Syglinde have had a small knife with her, such as ladies might use for their fancy work?''

"Aye, that she hath. I gave it her myself. 'Tis no longer than her sweetly tapered finger. She carrieth it always in a silken pouch slung from her waistband. How wot ye of the knife, bard?''

"If she'd had a bigger knife, she could have used it to defend herself and might not have got carried away. If she'd had none at all, she couldn't have cut off her hair to make this collar. That's a bright young woman you have there, Torchyld. As I see it, she meant this as a message to you. She's alive and kicking, but she's shut up some place where she can't get out. The griffin could and did, but not without a struggle. She helped him escape, and sent him to find you.''

"Noble Ffyff!''

Torchyld flung his arms around the griffin's neck and wept until the beast began to utter plaintive squawks at getting its head soaked. Torchyld wiped his eyes on the soft, red fur and composed himself.

"Turned him loose from where?''

"Oh, from the castle, I should think. Is there any room up in a tower or somewhere that has a lockable door and a window barely large enough for a griffin to squeeze out of? It must be high off the ground. I can't think of any advantage an old griffin would have over an active young woman, except its wings.''

Torchyld shook his head. "Ye castle windows be not large enow. Big windows invite attack.''

"I know that. But there must be one somewhere.''

Torchyld shook his head. "None. Save only," above his mustache and beneath his sunburn, he paled, "in ye tower of Ruis ye Accursed. But Syglinde would never go there!''

"Why not?"

"It be a direful place. None hath entered yon tower since Ruis was killed in years agone. His own men slew that wicked king to punish crimes too black for speaking, and walled up his body inside ye tower whence erst he hurled his victims to their doom after he had worked his evil will of them. His fearful ghost still walketh there. Great-uncle Sfyn was going to raze it to the ground, but Dwydd warned him against loosing ye wickedness encased therein."

"That so? Is this tower actually a part of the castle?"

"Woe unto us, it be."

"Would it be situated anywhere close to the banqueting hall?"

"Aye, bard, it leadeth up from ye west end of ye hall, but there be no door. Ye king's men blocked it in years agone with great stones that none dare move, and covered ye stones with a thick-woven arras."

"You don't say? Well, don't worry, Torchyld. At least we've got the griffin back, and we know Syglinde still has her wits about her. I do think we ought to press on to the castle as fast as we can, though. Is Ffyffnyr able to travel, do you think, Dan?"

"I should not advocate his attempting to fly with that broken wing feather, but his legs and talons appear to be in good order. If we find our pace too quick for him, I can stay behind and bring him along slowly. How far do we have to go?"

"Gin we start now, we could be there ere mid-morn, e'en carrying the archdruid's litter," Torchyld informed him.

"Then let us march," cried Huw. "Gin needs must, we can make a litter for ye griffin also."

Once up on his talons, though, Ffyffnyr himself set a pace that even Torchyld couldn't have bettered. The griffin seemed frantic to get to the castle. Not knowing anything about a griffin's mental powers but impressed by the instinct that had led Ffyffnyr to Torchyld, Peter was inclined to think it might behoove the rest of them to feel frantic, too.

By changing the litter bearers every hundred yards or so, they managed to keep up their speed. Even Daniel Stott, having the advantage of a longer stride than most, was galloping along for all he was worth. They hadn't been marching for more than an hour when they caught sight of the flag-hung battlements of King Sfyn's castle. All at once, the six sons of Lord Ysgard stopped short and looked a bit foolish.

"Now what do we do?" asked Yfor.

"Good question," said Peter Shandy.

Ffyffnyr, who'd paused only long enough to pant, answered him with a whine.

"Right, Ffyff," Shandy replied. "On your feet again, everybody. Forward, march!"

CHAPTER 13

The castle was a charming spectacle, set up on a rise inside its moat, framed in bright green grass and bright pink daisies, crowned with fanes and pennons bravely a-flutter against rough-cut gray stone battlements and turrets. As they paused at the edge of the woods to admire the view, the drawbridge dropped, the portcullis lifted, and they heard a clattering of hooves and a fanfare of trumpets. Peter motioned his group back into the trees.

"Wait a moment. Let's see who it is and what they're up to."

"Mine uncles," Torchyld murmured, "faring forth to hawk. See, they hold their falcons, their gyrfalcons, their merlins, and their peregrine eyas tiercels on their wrists."

And a brave company they made on their white and gray and roan and coal-black horses, with their red and blue and green cloaks streaming out behind them. Shandy could see the fierce birds, quiescent now in their colored leather hoods, the sun picking little glints off the tiny silver bells attached to the jesses on their legs. There were almost as many women as men in the group, and Shandy could feel the sighs of Lord Ysgard's six sons stirring the folds of his robe at sight of them.

He half-turned and motioned again for silence. This was a real stroke of luck. With so many of his relatives out of the way, Torchyld should be able to lead them into King Sfyn's presence with a minimum of fuss. That big man heading the hawking party looked like the sort to throw his weight around if he got a chance.

"Who's that one out in front?" he muttered to Torchyld.

"Mine uncle Edmyr, giving himself ye king's place already."

Shandy saw what Torchyld meant. It must be hard to strut on horseback, but Prince Edmyr was managing.

As the procession disappeared in single file into the forest path Torchyld identified them for Peter. "That be Uncle Edwy, and Aunt Edelgysa just behind him lest he stray too close to a lady-in-waiting. And Uncle Edbert and Aunt Gwynedd. I see not Aunt Aldora. She must have one of her headaches. And Cousin Dagobert looking glum, and Cousin Owain smirking all over his silly face, and Gelert and Gaheris. Those be all ye family. The rest be people of ye court."

"Good God, what's that old woman on the gray mule tagging along for?"

"That be Dwydd. She liketh well ye screams of ye dying when ye hawks pounce on ye prey."

Ffyffnyr was whimpering and straining, acting as if he'd like to pounce on somebody, too.

"All right," Shandy said as soon as the hunting party was out of sight, "let's move in."

"We ought to be in brave array like Prince Edmyr's party," Yorich fretted, "and mounted on great steeds instead of straggling along on foot like a pack of beggars. And we have no fanfare of heralds' trumpets to announce us as befits our rank."

"Stick out thy chest and blow thy nose," said Hywell. "We brought presents, didn't we? And we be fresh bathed and shorn. And we found ye griffin. How dost ye, old redcoat? Going to give me one of thy grifflets for a wedding present?"

Ffyffnyr started to rear up on his hind talons and flap his wings, but Daniel Stott ordered, "Down, sir," and he subsided. Still he was impatiently pressing forward, snuffling and whimpering like a bloodhound on the trail.

The drawbridge had been left down, no doubt for the hawking party's return. The walkers formed up and marched over it as bravely as they could, Torchyld leading the way with Ffyffnyr, Tim next in his litter looking dignified as all hell, Dan behind him still carrying his crozier and walking with firm, measured tread; and Peter bringing up the rear with the four young lords who weren't serving as litter bearers. Altogether they must have made an impressive enough showing; at least the sentries at the portcullis were sufficiently stunned.

"Sir Torchyld! Ye brought him back."

"Aye, but I didn't take him away. How be my great-uncle ye king?"

"His majesty be in parlous state, Sir Torchyld. He but sitteth on his throne with his mustache trailing in his metheglin, meaning no disrespect to his august person, fretting for Ffyffnyr."

"Then this really be Sir Torchyld, ye mighty wyvern-slayer, great-nephew of ye puissant King Sfyn. And we his comrades!" cried Yfor. The six sons of Lord Ysgard needed no panoply of horses and trumpets to boost their self-esteem as they swooped on into the banqueting hall.

And there, as reported, sat an old man, bent and melancholy inside his royal robes until Ffyffnyr, thrashing his wings and whoofling in ecstasy, hurled himself at the throne.

The reunion brought lumps to the throats of all present. Captains and corporals, scullions and minions came flocking. Then came an excited babbling of female voices and the granddaughters of King Sfyn rushed into the great hall, rustling their finery and smelling deliciously of rose-petal water.

"I want ye little redhead with ye freckles," yowled young Hayward, unable to contain his passion.

"Not yet," Torchyld snarled.

"But she wanteth me, too. I can tell by the way she batteth her eyelashes and twitcheth her ears."

"Ye have to be presented first. Protocol. Hoy, guards, let me through to ye throne. Ffyff, breathe some fire for ye king."

That sent them all scrabbling backward, giggling and applauding. Torchyld seized the diversion to re-form his squad. While Ffyffnyr was producing a veritable rainbow of sparks and flashes, with a cloud of royal blue smoke for an encore, Torchyld marched his friends up to his great-uncle.

"Oh, ye be back, be ye?" growled the king.

"Yea, I be back with Ffyff, rescued from dire peril and durance vile, and grateful to me even if ye be not. And I brought distinguished guests; and a bunch of husbands for ye girls, bearing rich presents and burning to woo. And where be my Syglinde?"

"One thing at a time, ecod. Who be ye most distinguished guest?"

"I be, dammit." Timothy Ames extricated himself from the litter and stretched out his hand. "Archdruid Timothy Ames at your service, sir. And this is Assistant Archdruid Dan Stott. And our head bard, Pete Shandy."

Murmurs of awe and wonder spread through the gathering as they watched the king perform the hitherto unknown ritual of the handshake with the archdruid, the assistant archdruid, and the bard. When the formality was completed, Tim brought forth the young lords.

"And we've got a bunch of lovesick swains here, panting to meet the young ladies. Sons of your neighbor Lord Ysgard, down the road a piece. They've got a woman shortage over there. You introduce 'em, Pete. I can't keep their names straight."

The six strapping young men lined up in front of the throne. Peter reeled off their names. Each made his reverence to King Sfyn, then beetled off to where Torchyld was doing the honors among his cousins. Luckily there were also six princesses, so nobody got left out, everybody fell in love at first sight, and all were then and afterward delighted with their choices. Peter was reminded of the grand finale of a Gilbert & Sullivan operetta.

Ah, but what of the leading man and the leading lady? Peter took a quick look around the throne room, nodded to himself, observed that everybody else was either making polite conversation, petting the griffin, or getting betrothed, stepped briskly around behind the throne, and vanished.

CHAPTER 14

"Pete! Pete, where the hell are you?" That was Tim's voice.

"He was here by my side not a moment ago." That was Dan's.

"He poofed." That was Torchyld's.

"Another vanishment," groaned King Sfyn, no doubt taking a firmer grip on Ffyffnyr, because Shandy could hear the griffin squeak. There must be tiny, hidden openings in the stonework. Ruis the Accursed had chosen his masons cleverly.

Too bad they hadn't invented chimneys while they were about it. Smoke from the fire in the banqueting hall, which probably never went out, had turned the staircase into a kipper factory. No doubt the allegedly impenetrable tower acted as a flue. That meant, as he'd suspected, there must be a good-sized opening up above somewhere. Christ, was there no end to these stairs?

At least there was an occasional slit in the outer wall. These let out a little of the smoke, and provided enough daylight for him to see where he was going, if anywhere. Peter stopped to get a whiff of fresh air and a squint at the country outside. Maybe this was the direction they'd come from. He couldn't tell; all he could see was that seemingly endless ring of dark green forest beyond the open plain and the moat. Full of unicorns and heffalumps, no doubt. Why shouldn't he believe in mythical monsters, considering he'd become so recently acquainted with his first griffin?

Not a bad critter, either. He wondered what Jane Austen, the family cat back in the little brick house on the Crescent, would think of sharing her kitty box with a grifflet. Not much, he suspected. Like most females, Jane had a well-developed sense of the territorial imperative.

Speaking of females, he'd better get on with his self-assigned task. Torchyld must be having fits by now. He struggled upward through the smoke and the mirk until at last he came to a heavy oaken door girt with bands of iron. It had a massive iron bar and a hook for the bar to rest in, but for some reason the bar was left hanging and the door secured with a billet of wood. He didn't stop to wonder why, but snatched the billet away and swung the door open.

"Lady Syglinde?"

"Don't ye Lady Syglinde me, ye old—Oh!"

Just in the nick of time, the blond fury lowered the empty wooden trencher she'd been about to brain him with. "Who be ye?"

"Peter Shandy, traveling bard," he informed her. "Sir Torchyld sent me."

"Torchyld? O name of love and gladness! Where be my valiant knight?"

"Downstairs in the banqueting hall, eating his heart out with longing for you."

"Then why came he not himself to get me instead of sending an emissary? Silly great ox that he be."

"He didn't know where to find you, that's all, and I did. He got your message, though. That was a clever stroke of work, young woman. Is this the window you let the griffin out of?"

Peter walked over and measured the aperture with his eye. "Must have been a tight fit."

"Aye, that it was. We struggled amain. Ffyff squirmed and I pushed. Poor old griffums, did he get his pretty fur skinned off?"

"Just a broken wing feather and a few minor abrasions. Care to be rescued?"

"Aye, I must fly to my darling. Would that I, too, had ye wings of a griffin. Let me go first, I pray."

"All right, but be careful. If you took a header down these stairs, you'd kill yourself. How in Sam Hill does that old crone go cavorting up and down here with her kidnap victims?"

"Dwydd? Ye have wrought her downfall?"

"Not yet, but I'm working on it. How did she get the pair of you up here?"

"Nay, I wot not. By some cantrip spell, meseems. I remember only feeling strangely befuddled, then being pushed into a dark place and being made to climb and climb until methought I should faint. When I got to the top, I swounded. Then somehow darling Ffyffnyr was stretched out on ye floor of that accursed room, snoring great snores that sent purple smoke out of his nostrils. I laid my head on his tummy for comfort as I used to when but a tiny tot. Then I knew no more until he woke me by licking my face with his great tongue, which is like a cat's but rougher."

"Did you know where you were?"

"There was a black thing over ye window so I could not see, but I tore it down. Then I realized where we must be, and I was sore afraid. Then I thought, Syglinde, ye great ninny, this be no time to play ye timid maiden, so I cut off a tress of my hair and braided it around Ffyff's neck and told him to go and find Torchyld, and he went. Ye have seen my darling with thine own eyne? Hath he any wound?"

"He claims his heart is sore with longing for you, that's all. He's had some—er—parlous gestes since you saw him last, but he acquitted himself nobly."

"He could do no other. Will this staircase never end?"

"Careful, now. Don't rush it. I think we're just about—listen!"

They must be almost down to the hall by now. Torchyld's voice came clearly through the wall, raised in frantic outcry.

"Damn it, Great-uncle Sfyn, where be she? I brought ye Ffyff, I want my Syglinde."

"Nay, I know not," the old man was quavering when Syglinde burst from behind the arras and flung herself into her hero's arms.

"My beloved!"

"My adored!"

Some things hadn't changed much over the centuries, Peter thought, watching the lovers replighting their troth. The six sons of Lord Ysgard, profiting by their example, started betrothing the six granddaughters of King Sfyn, and it was some time before the king could get a word in edgewise over the busses and osculations. At last he turned to Peter and bellowed in right kingly tone, "Bard, ye hast mighty powers. Gin it be not a trade secret, how didst work this disenchantment?"

"Easily enough, your majesty. Weren't you aware there's a staircase directly behind your throne, hidden by that arras?"

"Aye, I wist it well. But ye staircase hath long been blocked with stone and sealed with profound spells and deep curses."

"The hell it hath, with all respect to your royalty. Dwydd's been giving you the business."

"Ye words be strange, but ye meaning be clear, Bard Pete. That old besom shall be dealt with right royally when she returneth. But now 'tis time to celebrate ye return of my beloved griffin and my only somewhat less esteemed greatnephew, not to mention ye arrival of our distinguished guests and all this merry betrothing. Ho, minions! Fetch forth ye drinking horn and pile high ye banqueting board. Archdruid, prithee take ye place of highest honor at my right hand. Assistant archdruid, come and sit at my left hand. H'm, now who getteth to sit where? My daughter-in-law Edelgysa be wont to manage ye protocol, but she hath gone a-hawking. Ah, here cometh Aldora," he said with relief as a pale though still lovely woman entered the hall. "How goeth ye headache? Ye see our prodigals have returned."

"And, Mama, I be betrothed," cried young Princess Imogene. "This be Lord Yfor, eldest son of Lord Ysgard. Ye wottest, that place whence come all those kidnapped maidens. Be he not adorable? Look what he brought me."

She lifted her plump arm to display several handsome bracelets and gold rings. Her mother raised her eyebrows in pleased surprise.

"Welcome, Lord Yfor. Although I must say it would have been more seemly to ask Prince Edmyr and myself for her hand before making thy proposal."

"Oh, Mama, be not so stuffy," cried Imogene. "Nobody bothereth about those silly old customs nowadays. Anyway, Grandpa thinketh he be lovely. Dost not, Grandpa?"

"Eh?" King Sfyn squinted from under his enormous eye-brows at the young lord on whom Imogene was keeping so tight a grasp. "Yfor, eh? Wasn't it thy father who sent me that nasty message about wanting his wenches back? Threatened me with invasion, or some such nonsense."

"He was a trifle upset, sire. It be awful, trying to run a castle with no women. But that be all settled now, ben't it, Immie darling?"

"Mama, I've got one, too." Gwendolyn couldn't be kept back any longer. "This be Yorich. Dostn't just love ye way his teeth stick out?"

"Like hern," said Yorich fatuously.

Then all the nieces had to present their swains, amid much giggling and flouncing and wrangling over whose boy was the handsomest and whose girl the prettiest. In truth they were none of them anything to write home about beside Torchyld and Syglinde; but those two were off in a world of their own and didn't count.

The esnes and lackeys lugged in immense trenchers of baked meats, including a specially high-piled one of boiled eels for Ffyffnyr at which Daniel Stott gazed with some pertur-bation. However, the griffin slurped them down and, it may be said, suffered no ill effects then or later.

The drinking horn passed from hand to hand. The lovers flirted, the old king beamed, the griffin belched dainty red and pink heart-shaped sparks. All was joy and revelry, until the hunting party returned.

No longer was theirs a brave procession. The hawkers en-tered with bowed heads. In their midst came four men bearing a body on a litter. Prince Edmyr was no longer leading the show.

"Oh, God! My husband," shrieked Princess Aldora. She ran to the litter, caught up the prince's limp hands, and started chafing them frantically between her own.

" 'Tis no use, Aldora," said Prince Edbert. "His horse stum-bled and threw him headlong on a heap of stones."

"That cannot be! Ne'er was there horse Edmyr could not ride."

"Ye steed was bewitched," cackled the old hag in black, forcing her way to the front. " 'Twas thy great-nephew ye wicked sorcerer, O king. He lurked in ye woods to which ye banished him in quest of Ffyffnyr, whom I doubt not he hath by now slain in his wickedness. As Prince Edmyr's charger leaped forward, he arose from behind ye rocks and—"

"And what, ye old bag of lies?" roared the young giant.

"Sir Torchyld!" Dwydd reeled back, clutching at her wizened throat with a dirty yellow claw. "Aagh! Ye liveth not. Art but an evil apparition."

Syglinde laughed, a clarion ring of purest silver. "And ye art but a liar, nasty old crone. My Torchyld be no apparition! He hath been right here by my side. My ribs ache from his embraces and my arms from returning them. There be, I grant ye, enchantment in his kisses, but he casteth that spell only for me. And see, here be ye griffin ye claim he slew in his wickedness. Breathe a little fire for Dwydd, Ffyff darling."

The griffin obliged with a livid green eel-shaped tongue of flame darted straight at the witch. She reeled back in horror.

"Nay, this cannot be! 'Tis sorcery."

"It be no sorcery, silly witch. Thy wicked tricks be discovered. Here be wise and mighty druids whom my darling Torchyld brought back to rid us of thy vicious wiles."

"Then why did they not stop my husband from being killed?" sobbed Princess Aldora.

"Believe me, ma'am, we would have if we could," said Peter. "We are not magicians, only men trained to use the brains we were born with. All I can say is, if there's any ill-doing involved in your husband's death, we'll try to find it out."

"This be all lies and sorcery," Dwydd was still screaming.

Syglinde wasn't the girl to take any such nonsense. "Like ye lies ye told the king about Torchyld's stealing Ffyffnyr away, when all the time ye'd hidden him in the secret room at the top of Ruis's tower, where ye hid me, too. Ye be a stupid old baggage, Dwydd, and thy trickery worketh no more. Behold!"

She pulled away the arras from behind the throne, raising a cloud of dust and moths. The open doorway and the staircase behind it were plain to see.

"Ye release ye evil emanations," screamed Dwydd.

"Fiddle-faddle," Syglinde snapped back. "Ye only evil emanations around here come from thy unwashed carcass. There be nothing in that tower save rats and spiders, any one of whom hath a sweeter nature than thine."

"That reminds me," said Peter. "It may comfort you to know that your late friend Gwrach meant to send you a thank-you note. She was most grateful to you for sending her so fine a dinner as Sir Torchyld. As you see, however, she never got to eat him."

"Eat him?" cried Syglinde. "Torchy dearest, what meaneth this bard?"

"Oh well, ye see, we had this geste. Tell her, bard. Ye can put in all ye fancy touches."

"Be it seemly to be telling stories while my noble brother-in-law, heir to ye throne, lieth cold in death?" snapped a tall, commanding woman in a long green gown with a gold surcoat.

"Princess Edelgysa be right," sobbed the wretched Aldora. "First my son, and now my husband. I be indeed accursed."

"Ye still have me, Mother." A tall youth, handsome in a slim, poetic sort of way, carrying a hooded hawk on his wrist, came to put his other arm around his weeping mother.

"That be my cousin Dagobert," Torchyld murmured to Peter and his friends.

"Nice-looking boy," Tim grunted. "So he's next in line to the throne now? Hope his life insurance is paid up."

"M'yes," Peter murmured back. "Quite a coincidence, isn't it? I'd like to get a closer look at the body. Shall we perform a druidical rite?"

"How, for instance?"

"March around and look solemn, I suppose."

"Let Dan do it. He's solemner than I am."

"But you're the big cheese. It would show lack of respect to all this royalty if you didn't participate. Come on, Tim."

Peter stood up and addressed the king. "Your Majesty, the archdruid wishes to demonstrate his sympathy for you and your family by performing a brief but solemn rite, assisted by his assistant and myself. First, we suggest a bier be brought and the body of the lamented prince be laid on it according to your—er—usual custom."

"Yes, yes, a bier," cried Princess Aldora. "Ye bier that but one moon ago held my precious Dilwyn."

"I believe you said Dilwyn was in fact the elder brother?" Shandy asked Torchyld, who had momentarily come up for air.

Torchyld only blinked and smiled. Syglinde, however, still had a few of her wits about her. "That be so, Bard Pete. Dilwyn would have been crown prince now, were he alive."

"So I thought. And how did he and his brother get along?"

She shrugged, causing her pale blue gown to ripple bewitchingly. "Like brothers. Well enough, in their way. Though Dilwyn was the elder, Dagobert hath always been ye quicker. While yet a stripling, he excelled at swordplay and jousting. To ye day of his death, Dilwyn could ne'er remember which end of ye lance did ye lancing. He was a kind, gentle youth who craved only to lie on ye bank anext ye moat and pick out which eel he would eat for his supper."

"Did he actually catch these eels and have them cooked especially for him?" Peter asked.

"Nay, 'twas but a fancy. Dilwyn would eat any eel he could get. Like Ffyffnyr," Syglinde added with a fond glance at the wounded griffin, now asleep with its head lolling in the old king's lap.

"Liked his grub, did he?"

"Ate like a pig," grunted Torchyld. "Syggie, do ye have to keep talking all ye time?"

"Wouldst have me show disrespect to a learned bard?"

"I'd have ye show a little affection for thy conquering hero," said her betrothed, getting back to business.

"Stop it, great oaf, or I'll eat ye the way that sorceress tried to do." Syglinde snapped her teeth at his ear. They were nice, white teeth, Peter noted, and appeared to be all present in the right places. That fact alone would no doubt have established her as a beauty. "Was she pretty?"

"Hideous beyond belief," he reassured her. "Uglier than Dwydd, even. She had—" He whispered something, and Syglinde giggled.

"Silly! No woman hath that many."

"This was no woman."

"Can ye two not behave in a more seemly manner, in ye face of our terrible bereavement?"

That was Aunt Edelgysa handling the protocol again. Syglinde blushed prettily and straightened her disarranged bodice.

"I grieve for Prince Edmyr, in sooth, but he did pinch my bottom right oft."

Edelgysa's eyes narrowed. "Prince Edwy indulgeth in no such tasteless frivoling."

Lady Syglinde gave her a demure look and said nothing. By now the black-draped bier had been brought, and Prince Edmyr's body laid on it. Peter nodded to his friends and the three of them marched out toward it.

"What the hell are we supposed to be doing?" muttered Tim. "I feel like a goddamn fool. Sing something, can't you, Pete?"

"No," Peter muttered back. Nevertheless, he took a few swipes at the harp strings and decided to give it a shot.

"Another good hawk-toter has gone to meet his fate.
I hope he'll find a parking place inside the golden gate.
Another stall is vacant in the castle of King Sfyn
For Prince Edmyr's picked up his chips and sadly cashed
    them in."

"Great stuff, Pete," hissed the archdruid. "Keep it up."

Peter nodded, took a deep breath, and jangled another chord.

"The first to go was Dilwyn, a prince who loved to eat.
He scoffed his eels and hiked his heels straight to the
    judgment seat.
Now Pop has gone to join the throng across the Great
    Divide—
And barding is the stiffest job that I have ever tried.
So pardon me, fair company, if in a minor key,
I simply offer one and all my deepest sympathy."

Peter strummed one last, mournful discord, lowered his harp, and bowed his head. Daniel Stott, deeply moved, patted him on the shoulder.

"You clutch at the heartstrings, old friend. I should venture to estimate there is hardly a dry eye in the hall."

"Verily," observed a courtier standing nearby, "I have heard bards in my day, but ne'er one like this."

"These be strange and wonderful times we live in," agreed another. "Think ye they be really men, or enchanters?"

"Hell's flames, of course we're men," said the venerable archdruid, turning around and fixing the speaker with a baleful eye. "Button your lip or I'll turn you into a goddamn sheep and put you out to pasture. We're conducting a solemn rite, dammit."

Peter was, at any rate. He grew very solemn indeed as he noticed a small cut, with some bruising around it, at the base of Prince Edmyr's skull. It must be fresh, for there was a tiny trickle of dried blood still around it.

"Take a look," he muttered to the archdruid, "and tell me how a man could get a whack like this falling headfirst off a horse."

"It's not very deep," Tim grunted. "You don't suppose one of the hawks flew down and pecked him?"

"Someone would surely have observed such an occurrence," said Dan. "In any event, the beaks of raptors are adapted to tearing, not pecking."

"That's right," said Peter. "It looks to me more like the sort of mark that might have been made with a sharp pebble and a slingshot. Spang in the medulla oblongata. Might have been hard enough to stun him for a second. At the least, it would have given him one hell of a surprise. Distracted him, maybe made him drop the reins. If you plugged a man just as he was heading down a steep, rocky slope at a pretty good pace, for instance, you'd stand a reasonable chance of making him fall off. And," Peter added, feeling around inside the broad crimson hood that had been carelessly tossed back over the shoulders when they'd first seen the prince on horseback, "I shouldn't be surprised if this is what hit him."

"What is it?" Tim asked him.

"I'm not up on falconry, but I'd say it's one of those silver bells they tie on the hawks' legs."

"Cute."

The bell was a dainty thing, skillfully fashioned, with a tiny hole at the top for a thong to be threaded through. Dan Stott hefted it gently in his palm.

"This would have had to be from one of the larger birds, not a peregrine or a merlin, but a goshawk or gyrfalcon. Did Prince Edmyr hunt with such a bird?"

"Let's find out." Shandy took back the bell and stepped over to Prince Dagobert. "Can you tell me how this thing happened to get caught in the hood your father was wearing?"

"Nay, I cannot. It be a bell from one of ye hawks."

"I know, but which? Did the bird he was carrying lose a bell?"

"I cannot say, but I think not. My father would have waxed exceeding wroth gin anything had gone awry with ye accoutrements. And gin ye bell had been loose, would it not have fallen to ye ground rather than into ye hood?"

"Good point. He wasn't in the habit of carrying a spare one there, just in case it might be needed?"

"Not my father," Dagobert replied with an edge of bitterness Peter did not fail to note. "He would have expected one of his attendant gentlemen to carry it. Or me."

"Were you then carrying such a bell this afternoon?"

"Nay, not I. I doubt anybody was. It be not our custom."

"Your father was carrying a hawk earlier, I believe. What happened to the bird after he was thrown?"

A gentleman stepped forward. "Prince Edmyr was carrying no hawk when he fell, honored bard. He had been working with Hebog, our largest gyrfalcon, but he handed her to me as we commenced our homeward ride. She had both bells attached to her legs when I took her from him, and when I restored her to her block in ye hawkery."

"I see. Thank you. Can anybody else suggest how this bell might have got into Prince Edmyr's hood? Princess Aldora, can you help us?"

The stricken widow only shook her head. "I have never known him to put anything into his hood save his head, and that only in foul weather. He liked better a plumed hat, or his jousting helmet."

"He'd have liked best a crown," Dagobert muttered, so low that only the three men around the bier heard him.

"Were you riding beside your father on the way home?" Shandy asked the prince.

"I never rode beside my father. Always behind."

"How far behind? Were there other riders between you and him?"

"My uncles and my aunts. I was back among my cousins, and ye attendant lords and ladies."

"Could I see your cousins, please?"

Three young men stepped forward. Two were slender, brown-haired youths who looked a good deal like Dagobert himself. These were Gelert and Gaheris. The third was taller and more heavily built; black-haired, black-eyed, and handsome in a hot-eyed, heavy-lidded sort of way. If he'd been a woman, Peter thought, one might have called him sultry. This had to be Prince Owain, only son of Prince Edwy and Princess Edelgysa and clearly favoring his mother's side of the family. His smile was ineffably condescending.

"Do all bards ask so many questions about other people's concerns?"

Daniel Stott drew himself up in full majesty and raised his crozier by way of admonishment. "Peter Shandy is no ordinary bard. In his own country, he is famed for his ability to find out the truth when all others fail. He will ask any question if it serves his just purpose, and it behooves you to answer accurately, because he will surely find you out if you do not."

Owain's eyelids were raised in astonishment, then dropped again. "A veritable marvel among bards, forsooth. But what be there to find out? My uncle's horse stumbled, he fell forward, brast his neck, and died. All this ado about a silver bell from ye leg of a hawk may be interesting to a bard, but it be distressing to Prince Edmyr's father ye king, and to all of us who held our crown prince in due obeisance."

"My son speaketh well," said Princess Edelgysa.

"Your son speaketh too damned much," muttered Prince Dagobert, again not loudly enough for his aunt to hear.

Shandy was not a violent man, by and large; but he wouldn't have minded watching Prince Dagobert land his cousin a lusty buffet across the chops. He wouldn't have minded poking Owain himself, for that matter; but belting a prince was probably contrary to court protocol. He settled for a grave look and a stern voice.

"Madam, your son speaks as one who knows either too little or too much. Prince Owain, is your heart overruling your head, or vice versa?"

Ah, he'd managed to wipe that cocksure smirk off Owain's face.

"I wot not what ye mean," stammered the prince.

"I mean where were you when your uncle fell?"

"I was at ye rear with my cousins."

"Nay," said Prince Gaheris. "Ye were off to ye side with Lady Megan."

Shandy noticed Princess Edelgysa shooting a remarkably ill-tempered glance at a rosy-cheeked young woman who had a great deal of what it would no doubt take to interest a young fellow with a mouth like Owain's. Owain himself was glaring at Gaheris.

"She had a bee in her bodice. I but moved to assist her."

"She carrieth her own bee," snickered Gelert. "A noble geste, forsooth. Ye took a long time getting it out."

"How long a time?" Shandy demanded. "Was Prince Owain still engaged in this—er—apian pursuit at the moment Prince Edmyr fell?"

Gelert and his brother looked at each other and shrugged. "We cannot say. Our attention was drawn elsewhere."

"Where?"

"Someone up ahead cried out," Gaheris answered.

"Who did?"

"We thought it was our mother. Gelert said to me, 'Be that Mum?' "

"What was she crying out about?"

"Nay, we wot not," said Gelert. "We looked, but saw nothing amiss. Then our uncle's horse broke into a gallop and he fell off. After that, all was confusion. I myself had forgotten ye cry until ye asked and my brother mentioned it."

"That's why I find it necessary to keep asking," Peter told him. "It's natural to forget apparently trivial things in the face of a major crisis. Princess Gwynedd, can you tell me why you cried out?"

The young princes' mother, a petite and still delightfully pretty woman, shook her head until the heavy plaits of light brown hair flew. "I have no memory of so doing. I think I screamed when Prince Edmyr fell, but that was after. Mayhap 'twas one of ye hawks that screamed afore."

"Mother, I ken a hawk's scream when I hear it," Gaheris protested. "This was a woman."

"Mayhap Lady Megan found another bee," snapped Princess Edelgysa.

"Was it by any chance yourself who might have screamed, madam?" Shandy asked her.

"I? I never scream. I have no patience with weak vaporings. Have I, husband?"

"No, my dear," sighed Prince Edwy. " 'Tis true, honored bard. My wife screameth not."

"She bellows," muttered Prince Dagobert.

Dagobert could be quite a card, Peter thought, if somebody would only give him a course in assertiveness training. "Did you also hear this scream, Prince?" he asked.

"Perchance I did. It seemeth me somebody was always screaming. I paid no attention. I have had other things to think of since my brother's death."

"M'yes, I can see where you might have. And now you've a good deal more. Do you recall precisely where you happened to be in relation to other members of the party when your father fell?"

"I was beside my cousin Gelert, meseems."

"Not just then, Dag," his cousin contradicted, though gently. "I'd hung back a little to let Gaheris catch up. Ye were by yourself, more or less."

"Rather more than less, it appears. Thank'ee, Gel."

"Dag, did I say ilk thing to offend ye?"

"Not if it was the truth," Shandy interposed. "Prince Dagobert, this is a terrible time for you. Perhaps you'd prefer to—er—go off quietly with your mother for a while. You and I can have a private chat later."

"Nay," said the prince. "I prefer to remain. Contrary to what ye and some others of this court may be thinking, I wist not to seek this new responsibility. That fact doth not excuse me from facing it."

"Dagobert!" His mother looked up sharply. "What say ye?"

"I say only that I be now crown prince and it behooveth me to act ye part. Be that not so, Grandfather?"

"It be so, grandson," said the old king wearily. "I find some comfort in this direful moment to hear ye talking like a man."

"Prince Dagobert be perfect in this as in everything," Owain simpered with the exaggerated courtesy of a courtier.

Shandy gave Owain a thoughtful once-over. Jealous as hell. If it was motive anybody wanted, here was surely the likeliest candidate. The only difficulty was, how could Owain have spooked his uncle's horse if he was off in the underbrush fondling Lady Megan's erogenous zones at the time? He asked the lady.

"Do you recall precisely what was happening between you and Prince Owain at the moment when Prince Edmyr fell?"

"Prince Owain, having gallantly removed ye insect that was plaguing me, was then assisting me to regain my composure."

"How was he assisting you? Were both hands occupied in this—er—gallant effort?"

Lady Megan flushed bewitchingly and cast a nervous glance at Princess Edelgysa. "Of necessity they were, honored bard."

"And had been for some while?"

She nodded demurely. "Aye, noble bard."

"Prince Owain be ye soul of kindness," muttered Dagobert.

Prince Owain was out of the running as an assailant, anyway, unless this little minx was lying. She probably wasn't, mainly because she now realized certain other members of the hunting party had been taking an interest in her goings-on.

Too bad. Shandy would have enjoyed making that young jackanapes sweat a while. Furthermore, there was no gainsaying the fact that within a short week or so, Owain had moved from fifth to fourth to third in line for the throne, with only Prince Dagobert and his own father ahead of him.

And what of Prince Edwy, furthermore? At the moment, he appeared to be seeking solace in a drinking horn. Edwy looked like kind of a weedy cuss to Shandy. Maybe, like Dagobert, he wasn't totally overjoyed at suddenly being shoved up the ladder. But maybe that battle-ax wife of his wanted to be queen. Or maybe his youngest brother Edbert had got tired of being low man on the totem pole. Or maybe Torchyld was right about old Dwydd's wanting ultimate sovereignty even if she had to bump off the entire court to get it.

Peter had a hunch he wasn't going to learn anything worthwhile until he managed to get some of these people by themselves. Nevertheless, he went on patiently asking questions. The answers he got were tiresomely similar. Everybody could vouch for somebody, in all cases but one. Only Dagobert had no positive witness to his having remained sunk in thought, as he claimed, throughout the ride.

And Dagobert was, without a doubt, a capable young man. And Dagobert had resented his father, and had been deeply unsettled by his brother's death, or so it appeared from what he'd said. And Dagobert, judging from those muttered asides, was more the type to pull a sneak attack than to risk a bold confrontation. It looked as if they'd have to keep a wary eye on Dagobert.

CHAPTER 15

"I suppose you could call it social schizophrenia," Peter remarked to Dan Stott a little while later.

Everybody knew perfectly well that Prince Edmyr ought to be mourned as befitted his rank; everybody was willing to sympathize with the bereft Aldora and the new crown prince. Yet the sons of Lord Ysgard hadn't come to wallow in doom and gloom, nor had even the late Edmyr's own daughters any intention of putting a damper on the prenuptial festivities.

"What we must do," King Sfyn decided after another beaker of metheglin or two, "is to get these young minxes of ours married off with all dispatch. Then ye young lords can get back to guarding our neighbor Lord Ysgard's castle, and ye rest of us can get on with our grieving in accordance with usual court protocol. It cometh hard to compose ye mind to sad reflection when ye ear heareth all that squealing and smacking."

"True, wise father," said his son Edwy, who had been silently addressing himself to the drinking horn. "Let them go off to honeymoon in a happier place, then come back when ye mourning period is over and we can merrymake to their hearts' content. Can't do it now. Unseemly. Besides, perchance getting her daughters ready to be wed will take Aldora's mind off Dilwyn and Edmyr. Give her a grandchild to look forward to."

"If she hath not one already in ye making," sniffed Princess Edelgysa, with a scowl in the direction of her niece Imogene. Prince Yfor was demonstrating what a thoughtful husband he intended to be, by making sure Imogene didn't have a bee in her bodice.

"A sound decision," Peter agreed.

The princesses and the young lords all had ironclad alibis

for the time of Prince Edmyr's death. They'd been right here at the castle participating in a whirlwind mass betrothal. The sooner they were all out from underfoot, the easier it would be for him to get on with the investigation. Furthermore, Peter was enough of a prude to agree with what King Sfyn was no doubt really thinking. The sooner this collective union was legitimized, the less complicated it might become picking out eligible successors. At the rate the supply of currently available princes was running out, Sfynfford could before long find itself needing another generation of heirs.

As for Ysgard, it was entirely possible Lord Yfor might already have a job waiting for him back home. Peter was none too sanguine about the success of any geste that had Medrus at the head of it; at least not so far as Lord Ysgard was concerned. The ex-glow might have picked up a few of Gwrach's tricks.

Peter wouldn't have minded settling down in a corner for a quiet ponder on the possibilities, but Syglinde was clamoring for his support in petitioning the king.

"Gin all ye princesses are to be wed, may not Torchyld and I also be united at the same time? We have been betrothed so long."

"And so often," murmured Dagobert, loudly enough this time to raise a small gale of giggles from the princesses and their lovers.

"But then ye will leave me, to build thine own castle," the old king protested.

"And Torchyld will set up his own kingdom, belike," Owain drawled in that languid, teasing way; showing that while he pretended to joke, he meant to be taken seriously.

"Nay," roared Torchyld. "Gin I be lord of mine own demesne or disenchanted ex-apprentice bard, King Sfyn hath my sworn fealty. And so will King Dagobert. And, faith, he may need it gin able-bodied relatives be still swaggering around his banqueting hall fattening themselves on his bounty and plotting how best to undermine his puissance, instead of getting up off their rumps and going on gestes of their own."

"Brave words from a poor relation," snapped Princess Edelgysa.

"From an erstwhile poor relation," Torchyld reminded her. "Unless somebody hath been plundering ye king's treasure house in mine absence."

"Fool, dost not know ye law of Sfynfford? Any spoils of war won in ye king's service belong to ye king, to be divided among his lieges as he seeth fit. Wouldst rob an old man?"

"Wouldst let ye old man reign, woman?" barked King Sfyn. "I be none so feeble that I need my daughter-in-law to rewrite ye laws of ye kingdom according to her own convenience. Since when doth a wyvern's hoard count as spoils of war? When my son Edwy slew yon dragon that held ye prisoner, did I insist he share ye amongst my liegemen, forsooth? Torchyld hath made rich gifts to his kin, as a hero should. The rest of his wealth be his own, to spend as he chooseth. Yea, great-nephew, ye shall wed our beloved Syglinde. Ye shall choose land where ye wist, so it be not too far from me. There build ye a lordly manor house and live as befits ye rank and dignity of a king's great-nephew, and beget strong sons to serve ye chiefs of our line as valiantly as ye have served me. Doth mine answer please ye, Lady Syglinde?"

"Aye, dearest liege. And Torchy and I shall invite ye over for a weekend as soon as we have a roof to put over ye, and then our great-great grandchildren will be able to boast, 'King Sfyn slept here.' "

"Ah, dear fosterling, dost think future generations will ken or care who old King Sfyn was? E'en poor Ffyffnyr will be forgotten," he added mournfully, rubbing his hand over the graying muzzle.

"Not Ffyffnyr," said Peter Shandy.

In his mind's eye, he could see the souvenir shop outside his hotel: griffins on coffee mugs, griffins on neckties, on plastic notebook covers, on souvenir maps, on teacups, on aprons, on God knew what. Even the cardboard coaster on the pint he'd never got to drink in that misbegotten pub would have had a scarlet griffin printed on it.

"I predict," he said, "the day will come when it will hardly be possible for anybody to travel a mile throughout the length and breadth of this land without coming upon at least one likeness of Ffyffnyr."

"Can such a thing be possible?"

"Ask Assistant Archdruid Stott. He's the animal expert."

"My colleague does not err, Your Majesty," Stott assured the king. "Ffyffnyr's semblance will appear on flags and coats of arms. The red griffin will be honored as the symbol of an entire nation."

King Sfyn beamed. Ffyffnyr burped a few royal blue and purple flames, then went back to sleep.

"He be such a sweetie," sighed Syglinde. "Would we could but have a little Ffyff of our own in our new home. Torchy darling, dost suppose there might somewhere fly a nice red lady griffin whom Ffyffnyr would like to meet? E'en mayhap a pretty pink-and-white one?"

"Grandpa," cried Gelert. "I crave a boon. As soon as we get our sisters married and Uncle Edmyr buried, can Gaheris and I go on a geste to find a wife for Ffyff?"

"Perchance, lad. Ye decision must await our royal pleasure until more urgent affairs have been transacted. Let ye chapel be made ready for the lying-in-state of Prince Edmyr's body, then bedeck ye banqueting hall with flowers and rich hangings for the wedding. 'Tis indeed a confusing state of affairs. Let us be thankful ye archdruid be here to perform ye ceremonies in all good order."

"Huh?"

Timothy Ames, who had been refreshing him'self in a light doze, jumped awake as if he'd been zapped with a bean-blower. "Who, me? Don't you have a resident friar of orders gray, or a chaplain of the regiment, or somebody? I can't go muscling in on the local man's territory."

"We have only a smelly old hermit who liveth in a hut and maketh offensive suggestions to any woman who passeth by," Syglinde protested. "I will not be wed by ye likes of him."

"Nor I," cried Imogene, Gwendolyn, Guinevere, Gwladys, Aloisa, and Blodeuwedd in order of precedence. Tim realized he was in for it.

"Cripes, I better hold a conference with my boys. Excuse us, folks."

He beckoned Dan and Peter over to a neutral corner. "What the bloody flaming hell do we do now? I can't go around marrying and burying all this goddamn royalty. I wouldn't even know what to say. Hell, if I could have heard what the minister was getting at when he asked me to say 'I do' to when I married Jemima, do you think I'd have been fool enough to say it?"

Daniel Stott cleared his throat. "As it happens, I am well acquainted with the marriage ceremony, having gone through it with both Elizabeth and Iduna, not to mention my eight children's weddings. Furthermore, I have personally united twenty-seven couples in lawful wedlock."

"I'll be switched! How come?"

"My beloved father was, in addition to being a prominent pig farmer, our community's only justice of the peace. During one especially busy week in June, he contracted laryngitis. Rather than disappoint the large number of would-be brides and grooms, many of them also expectant parents, who had scheduled their nuptials for that auspicious time, he swore me in as assistant justice and had me perform the rites for him."

Peter Shandy rubbed his chin. "Er—Dan, how long ago did this swearing-in take place?"

"You raise a nice legal point, my friend. It would seem to me, however, that since we are now in the kingdom of Sfynfford, we are subject only to the local ordinances. Therefore, if we can obtain the king's formal permission, we may venture to perform a civil, though of course not a religious ceremony. As to the funeral, I submit that our qualifications, or lack of them, will probably make little difference to Prince Edmyr at this juncture. Therefore, we have but to manage the affair in such a way as to offer comfort and reassurance to the bereaved."

"And it would seem to me Dan's hit the nail on the head," said Tim with immense relief. "Okay, boys, let's tackle His Highness."

King Sfyn was somewhat puzzled at being asked to repeat, "By virtue of the power vested in me as high king of Sfynfford,

I hereby grant Daniel Augustus Stott official permission to perform marriage and funeral ceremonies at my court," but the formality made the three visitors feel easier. As for the young people, they were delighted that the stately assistant archdruid instead of his no doubt more distinguished but physically less impressive superior would get to officiate.

Thus was one rubicon temporarily bridged, if not yet crossed. Shandy left Tim and Dan to hoist a flagon with the old king in honor of the swearing-in, and beckoned Torchyld out of the hall. Syglinde came, too, since neither was willing to let the other out of sight.

"What be thy pleasure, honored bard?"

"I want you to show me the hawk house."

"The hawk house? Mean ye ye mews?"

"I suppose so. Why the mews?"

" 'Tis where we mew them up, in sooth."

"Ah, yes. It had slipped my mind that the word mews can mean something other than the noise cats make."

"In Sfynfford, cats say 'miaow.' " Syglinde made a delightful cat. She was in wild spirits now, laughing up at Torchyld and down at Peter, looking more ravishing than ever.

Peter didn't feel much like laughing back. He was finding the mews a daunting sort of place. He admired hawks, both for themselves and for their efficiency as unpaid hired hands on farms. However, he preferred to watch them soaring above the turnip fields, adjusting their marvelously engineered wings to the updrafts while they watched for field mice among the leaves. Sitting here silent on their perches with those leather hoods covering their heads, they looked too much like a row of executioners. He supposed that was what they were, from the mice's point of view.

Each bird had its own wooden stall, with a block to perch on and a screen of rough homespun to hang down over the opening to keep it warm and quiet, he supposed. The hawks' accommodations were probably superior to the resident hermit's, and a good deal cleaner. Dan would be relieved to hear how well they were looked after.

He walked around, trying to take inventory without getting

too close to those ominous talons. Each buteo and falcon appeared to have its two silver bells firmly attached to the leather strips around its legs. Some birds were tied to their perches by their jesses. Others were allowed to move about freely, although at the moment none of these was taking advantage of its privilege.

"They know they risk being struck gin they fly too close to another whilst hooded," Torchyld explained. "It be safer to stay in their own stalls, so they mostly do."

"Smart birds," said Peter. "Which is Hebog, the one Prince Edmyr was working with?"

"This be she, ye great gyrfalcon. Go not anigh. She striketh like a wyvern. Hebog be commander of ye mews. All ye rest be sore afeared of her."

"M'yes, I can see why."

Peter thought he himself might experience a mild perturbation of spirit if that damned great mass of feathers and fury swooped at him with her claws hooked out. Even tied and hooded, Hebog looked hardly more amiable than a wolverine with a sore paw.

"She's a good deal larger than any of the others, isn't she?" he remarked. "Don't you have any male gyrfalcons?"

"Aye, here be one." Torchyld pointed to a falcon that looked much like Hebog but was only about two thirds her size. "Wist ye not ye females be much bigger than ye tiercels?"

"Certainly I wist," Peter replied testily, although in fact he hadn't even known a tiercel was a male hawk until just now. "The light isn't too good in here, that's all. What I'm mainly interested in finding out is whether any of these birds has lost a bell. Help me double-check them, will you?"

Peter was hoping he'd overlooked an unbelled leg, but he hadn't. The master of the hawks, a likable cuss named Murfynn, came in with some fresh meat for the birds' suppers while they were searching. He assured them none was missing, and then showed them the box in which spare bells were kept.

"Behold, honored bard, all be in their places. We keep one pair for each class of bird. Some be larger, some be smaller, but in no case have we here a single bell."

Peter nodded. "I see. Very neat. I don't suppose there's any chance somebody could have—er—stolen a pair without your knowing?"

Murfynn drew himself up to his full height, which Peter estimated at four feet, six and a half inches. "Steal from King Sfyn? Nay, sire. It be not ye done thing."

"Urrgh," Torchyld agreed. "All ye bells we own be either on ye birds or in yon box. Gin more be needed, they must be cast by ye silversmith. Thus hath aye been ye custom."

"I see. So that would mean they always follow the same pattern."

"Aye, we have but ye one set of molds."

Peter took the silver bell he'd found in Prince Edmyr's hood out of his sleeve, where he'd had it tied up, and passed it to the master of hawks. "Then would you have any idea at all where this bell might have come from?"

Murfynn examined the trinket with keen professional interest, then shook his head. "Nay, sire, I wot not. This be none of ours."

He reached into his box and took out a bell of comparable size. "See, ours be more squat in shape, and hath a groove around ye middle. Wilt please ye to step outside into ye sunlight for a better look?"

"Thank you," said Peter, and stepped.

Now that he could make out the details, Peter had to agree with Murfynn. There could be no mistaking this bell for one of King Sfyn's. As a final check, he went around again, comparing it with the bells on the birds' legs and the ones from Murfynn's box. All the ones that should be identical were, allowing for the differences in their sizes to correspond with the varying weights of their wearers. None was at all like the one he'd brought with him.

"You're absolutely right, sir," he told Murfynn at last. "It doesn't even come close. So that still leaves us stuck with the question of how it got into Prince Edmyr's hood. Do you think it might have come off a hawk that escaped from some other owner and strayed into King Sfyn's territory?"

"Indeed, sire, I doubt it. That would be far to stray. And

were a belled hawk to appear in ye forests of Sfynfford, our woodmen would hear its chime and set nets to take it alive, supposing ye bird to be one of our liege's. And I should know gin they caught it, or heads would roll. Also, noble bard, ye may note this bell be not discolored from lying out of door, but simply darkened with time and lack of rubbing. Ours be bright as stars."

"So they be," Peter agreed. "You maintain a taut mews, sir. My compliments, and thank you for your time."

Murfynn saluted smartly. Shandy gave him a pleasant nod and went outside, where Syglinde and Torchyld had decided to wait.

"Good man," he remarked.

"Aye," said Torchyld. "Murfynn wotteth well his hawks. Where hie we next, Bard Pete?"

"You tell me," Peter groaned. "Does either of you have the faintest glimmering of a notion where in blazes this bell might have come from?"

Lady Syglinde nodded her exquisite head. "Perchance I can find ye a mate to it, gin it please ye. Torchy darling, prithee take Bard Pete to ye treasure room. I will meet ye there anon."

"Ye leave me, love?" cried Torchyld. "Whither goest?"

"To ask King Sfyn to bring ye key, dearest oakenhead, so we can get in. I shall tell His Highness my betrothed be desirous of choosing me a wedding present."

Laughing, she ran off. Torchyld stood gazing at her, so utterly besotted that Peter had to give him a few pokes in the ribs to remind him of the business at hand.

"Which way to the treasure room?"

"Ungh? Oh, past ye portcullis and turn right at ye donjon keep. Ye can't miss it."

"Aren't you coming, too? Lady Syglinde told us to meet her there, in case you'd forgotten."

"Lady Syglinde." Torchyld reached down casually and grabbed Peter by the throat. "Dost admit my lady to be beyond compare, bard, or do I feed ye to ye eels in ye moat?"

"I admit it freely," Peter managed to gurgle. "In fact, I'll be glad to spit in the eye of anybody who says she isn't, if you'll kindly ease up on my windpipe long enough to let me catch my breath. Furthermore, Lady Syglinde is not only beautiful, but intelligent."

"She be what?"

"She thinketh, my boy. She hath great store of brains packed into that gorgeous noggin of hers. You're a lucky ex-bard, in case you don't know it. Now get that blasted paw away from my gullet, and let's go see what she's hatching up in the family vault."

CHAPTER 16

The strong room looked impregnable enough. Its oaken door was even thicker, even more iron-bound than the one behind which Peter had found Lady Syglinde imprisoned back in Ruis's tower. Instead of a mere bar, it had a keyhole big enough to stuff a weasel through. Old King Sfyn must need a wheelbarrow to tote the key, Peter was thinking, when Syglinde showed up alone, carrying not only a wrought-iron key the size and heft of a crowbar, but also an armload of slates.

"Here, Torchy," she panted. "His Highness saith to take ye key and unlock ye door thyself. He be busy telling griffin stories to ye assistant archdruid. Ye end with all ye funny bumps on it be ye one that goeth into ye keyhole. Then ye turn until something clicketh, then ye open."

Torchyld took the key rather gingerly and spent considerable time trying to fit the wards into the lock wrong side up. At last he snarled, "Here, Bard Pete. 'Tis work for a wizard, not a warrior."

Peter accomplished the feat in a trice, thus earning their amazed reverence. In fact, the lock had been a cinch to open. It moved so easily despite its size that he decided it must have been oiled not long before. With eel grease, if his nose failed him not. The weighty door swung at a touch, without a sound. Oiled hinges, too. The castle maintenance man must have been on the job.

Torchyld entered first. Syglinde held high the rushlight she was carrying, somehow, along with her other impedimenta, and motioned Peter inside with a sideways nod of her head.

His first reaction was, "Holy cats! That wyvern must have kept its mind on its job."

For at least the past three centuries, from the look of things.

The three oaken coffers that presumably held King Sfyn's own treasure were outshone by a shoal of eel baskets, all of them heaped high with gold and silver, copper and bronze, and jewels of every shape and color.

"Looks as if you won't be hurting for the price of a meal yet awhile," Peter told the young knight with typical Yankee enthusiasm. "Not bad at all, for a young fellow just starting out. But how in Sam Hill are we supposed to find one measly little hawk bell among all these gold eyeball-gougers and diamond-studded maces? How do you know you've even got one?"

Syglinde shuffled among her pile of slates, and pulled out one of them.

"We have thus many."

She pointed to the slate, on which she'd drawn—and even Torchyld would have had to admit drawing was not Syglinde's outstanding talent—what was presumably meant to be a falcon. Beside the hieroglyphic were a dozen or so little scratches.

"I wot not of writing or numbers," she confessed prettily, "so I scratched a mark for each bell, and scratched a bird to show whereof I scratched."

"Great Scott," cried Peter. "Then all these slates mean you've taken inventory of the whole shebang?"

"Aye, gin ye mean we made a record. Torchy sorted into these eel baskets all ye armlets and necklets and plates and cups and different things, and I made scratches. See, here be an arm with a bracelet, and here be scratches, one for each bracelet. And here be a hand with a ring, and these be ye scratches for rings. Was this not ye right way to do, Bard Pete?"

"It's an excellent way. Which of you thought of it?"

"We thought of it together. Torchy said how ye hell were we going to remember how much we had of what, and I said mayhap we could keep track as children do when playing a game. See, gin we give or spend a piece, I will scratch off ye scratch for that piece. Torchy made rich presents to King Sfyn and to all his aunts and uncles and cousins when he brought home ye wyvern's hoard so we did not count those. And now we must pick out wedding gifts for our cousins. Dost think Immie would like this necklace of blue stones, Torchy dearest?" Syglinde wondered, picking up a few thousand dollars' worth of rough-cut sapphires set in heavy gold.

"Er—could we get this little matter of the hawk bell settled before you go on to the wedding presents?" Peter suggested.

"Hawk bell. Where did we put ye hawk bells, Torchy? There were but a few pair. Oh, I know. In a little leathern bag here among ye coins. I will spill them out on this treasure chest. A pair for a peregrine, a pair for a merlin, a pair for a harrier, a pair for a—no, that be not a pair. Where be its mate?"

"I expect this may be the mate, right here," said Peter, producing the one he hadn't been able to match up at the hawkery.

"Unless there be still another here," said Torchyld, fussing with the dainty bells.

"I don't see how, if you started out with pairs. You're one short, you know."

Peter, who loved to count things, had already totted up the number of bells spread out on the chest against the number of scratches on Lady Syglinde's slate. According to her tally, there should be sixteen. He saw only fifteen, not counting the one that had hit Prince Edmyr.

"Looks to me as if somebody's been dipping into the till, Torchyld. Why don't we try another batch? These jeweled necklaces, for instance. Chances are if somebody was looking for a few easily portable souvenirs, he'd pick these because they're probably the most valuable."

As it turned out, Peter was right. After they'd spent half an hour or so checking against the slates, Torchyld found he was the poorer by three necklaces, one of which Syglinde remembered well and was none too happy about because it had stones like dewdrops sparkling in the morning sun and she'd been planning to knock everybody's eyes out with it at her wedding. They'd also lost three rings, two massive bracelets, and seven loose stones as big as hens' eggs. Syglinde thought they might have been green ones but couldn't be sure as she hadn't yet figured out how to draw colors. In any event, it had been a tidy haul for somebody. Peter could readily understand why Torchyld and Syglinde were deciding to take a strong line about the theft.

" 'Tis not ye done thing to rifle a king's treasure room," said Torchyld severely. "Great-uncle Sfyn will go up in smoke when he heareth of this fell deed. 'Tis noble to give, but wicked to take without leave. So hath it aye been in Sfynfford, and so shall it be or I'll have ye guts of him that robbed me."

"An 'twas not a him, Torchy dearest?" Lady Syglinde suggested. "Bethink ye who hath caused us so much grief."

"Dwydd, by all ye powers of darkness! Accursed hag, where be she now? I will tear her foul carcass to shreds and feed ye bits to Hebog."

"And Hebog will get pains in her belly and Murfynn will be furious, silly."

"Then I will—Syggie, what be I to do?"

"I think ye should be guided by Bard Pete, whose wisdom surpasseth mine in e'en so great a measure as my beauty surpasseth his, darling ox-brain. Bard Pete, how shall we punish Dwydd and get my dewdrop necklace back?"

"Good question," said Peter. "I'd say our first step is to make sure it was in fact Dwydd who swiped the swag. Where do you suppose we're most likely to find her right now?"

"Skulking in her turret, belike," said Torchyld, "thinking up greater evils."

"Which way is the turret?"

"Bard Pete," gasped Lady Syglinde, "we cannot go there. She hath ye place guarded by ugly basilisks and foul demons."

"And old King Ruis with his head tucked underneath his arm, no doubt. I'm not impressed by Dwydd's bogles. Lead the way, Torchyld. You needn't come with us if you'd rather not, Lady Syglinde."

"Nay, whither Torchy goeth, I go. Shall I leave ye slates here?"

"No, it may be the part of prudence to keep them with you. Does anybody other than ourselves know you're keeping this tally?"

"Nobody. They would laugh and call it silly. And snatch away ye slates to scale from ye battlements, belike."

"I shouldn't be a bit surprised. You stick to those slates like glue, young woman, until you and Torchyld get that treasure safely into a strong room of your own. Let's have that key again. I want to make sure we leave this room locked up as tight as we can make it. Doesn't King Sfyn usually keep a guard posted here?"

"Nay, who would steal from ye king?"

"Good question. Does he sleep with that blasted great lump of iron every night? It must be hellish hard under his pillow."

Syglinde managed a nervous giggle. "Nay, Bard Pete, he hangeth ye key on ye same hook as his crown. With Ffyffnyr guarding ye door, none dare go in to take it away lest they be rent in twain."

"Except that Ffyffnyr's been off the job those past couple of nights. I wonder whether that's why he got poofed in the first place, or if somebody merely took advantage of the fact that the griffin wasn't around. It must have been somebody with plenty of gall, though, to stroll into the king's bedroom, collect the key and rob the strong room, then sneak the key back without being detected. Old people like him don't sleep all that soundly, as a rule. Could somebody have slipped a Mickey into his metheglin?"

"Be that a spell to make one sleep?" Torchyld asked.

"I expect you might call it that," Shandy conceded. "No doubt a similar effect could be obtained with a—er—posset of herbs. Do you grow any camomile around these parts?"

"Herbs be women's work. Syggie, what be camomile?"

"Nay, I wot not. But we do have herbs to calm and soothe. Like poppy, to rub on ye gums of sweet babes when their tiny teeth be trying to come out. We must plant abundance of poppy, Torchy darling."

"Drat it, Torchyld," said Shandy, "get your lecherous paws off that wench and attend to the business at hand. Lady Syglinde, I'll thank you to quit seducing a man while he's on the king's errand."

"Be ye on ye king's errand, sweetest one?" murmured that

Cymric Delilah, running her fingertips across her lover's lips with predictable results.

"Of course he is, damn it," Peter snapped. "It's King Sfyn's strong room that's been robbed, even if it was your treasure that got stolen."

"Right," said Torchyld, reluctantly loosing his grasp on his bride-to-be. "Cease toying with my fealty, Syggie, lest I clap ye into ye guardhouse."

"With all they drunken soldiers?"

"Sir Torchyld, I command you in the king's name to stop tickling that young woman," Peter ordered sharply.

Enough was enough. He glared at them balefully until at last he managed to get their natural urges under control and start them climbing the turret stairs.

This was another of those narrow, twisty ones. Drat it, why did Dwydd always have to conduct her perfidious operations from the higher levels? And how did that old hag manage to mount these confounded stairs without fracturing her rheumatics? Flapped up on a broomstick, maybe. It would have to be a short one, there wasn't much flapping room here. It was a good deal like crawling up a vertical drainpipe. He just hoped she was in. He'd hate to have sprung his Achilles tendons in vain.

Dwydd was at home. Her door was shut, but when they tried pounding on it, they could hear mutterings and scufflings within.

Syglinde risked Shandy's renewed displeasure by cowering close to Torchyld. "Be that a basilisk?" she whispered fearfully.

"It's just the old woman trying to unhook her corsets," Shandy replied firmly. This was no time for hysterics, unless he decided to throw a fit himself, which was not outside the bounds of possibility.

This door was all of wood, he noticed; the first one he'd come to in the castle that wasn't bound with iron. Even the hinges were of leather. Peter remembered the billet of wood that had been used to fasten the door of Syglinde's prison when there was a perfectly usable iron bar already available, recalled something he'd run across in a fairy tale at the age of nine, and nodded to himself.

"Open up in the king's name," he yelled.

After some more yelling and pounding, he got a reply.

"Who braveth ye wrath of mine guardian ghouls?"

"Shove it, Dwydd," he howled back rudely. "Your guardian ghouls are dead ducks. Open this door or we'll break it down."

Sullenly, the resident hag at last obeyed. "What seek ye with Dwydd?"

"We seek ye gold and jewels ye stole from my treasure trove," Torchyld roared.

That appeared to surprise her. "Nay, I stole naught. Think ye I durst enter ye king's strong room?"

"Think ye ye durst lie to me, hag? Confess!"

"Wait a moment," said Peter. "I think we can establish the truth on more—er—scientific lines. Here, Dwydd, this is for you."

He held out the huge iron key. She shrank away, shrieking.

"Arrgh! Take it away. Touch me not with that thing, else I die."

"M'yes, I thought so."

Peter let the key dangle from his hand. "You see, boys and girls, iron in any form is an effective charm against witches. Dwydd might not scruple to rob the king's strong room if opportunity presented itself, but what in fact she would not dare do is steal the key to unlock the door. She's more afraid of the key than she is of the king. Right, Dwydd?"

He raised the heavy iron instrument again. The evil crone scuttled back inside her fantastically cluttered den, picked up a dried bat, and began fanning herself frantically with its wings.

"I beg ye, sir bard, torture me no longer. I be old and frail and not ye witch I used to be."

"Then tell us all you know about the robbery."

" 'Tis easily told. I know nothing."

"Who talked you into kidnapping Lady Syglinde and Ffyffnyr?"

" 'Twas mine own idea," Dwydd answered sulkily.

"It's risky business lying to me, old woman. Why did you try to murder Sir Torchyld, first by blunting the edge of his sword before he went to kill the wyvern, and then by forcing him by means of your alleged enchantments and your galloping hogweed to face Gwrach unwarned and unarmed?"

"Nay, sire, I meant not to kill him, only to prove his mettle. I perceived what valor was in him, and wanted only to bring it out. And what happened? He be now famous throughout ye land, wealthy beyond compare, and about to wed ye most beautiful woman in ye kingdom. And all this he oweth to me. Had I not done as I did, he would still be marching up and down ye battlements cursing our monarch for not letting him marry his mistress or go on a geste to seek his fortune. And what thanks do I get? Threats and revilings. Pah!"

"Frankly, that's one aspect of the situation that hadn't occurred to me," Peter replied. "I'm sure it hasn't occurred to Sir Torchyld either, much less to Lady Syglinde, whom you sought to destroy by shutting her up in that so-called haunted tower. Nor do I believe any of us is ready to buy it now. Shall I repeat my question? Have you been running your own dirty tricks campaign, or has someone else been putting you up to it?"

Dwydd waved the bat in a wild arabesque, and bared what few teeth she had left. "Ye have mine answer. Take it or leave it. Only begone forthwith, lest I loose a mighty spell to blast ye."

"Oh, put down that silly bat and talk sense, woman. You can't scare me with your spells."

"I scared ye with mine hogweed," Dwydd shouted, hurling the bat at him.

"Come to think of it, so you did. All right, madam, that was one round to you. I trust you realize you're not going to win another, and I strongly advise you to reconsider your position. Allow me to return your bat."

CHAPTER 17

The all-wooden door slammed shut. Peter turned to his companions.

"Come on, you two. No sense wasting any more time here. She's not going to talk."

"Ye could have tortured her with ye key," Torchyld protested.

"No, I couldn't. It's contrary to protocol."

Shandy's personal protocol, anyway. He still felt queasy every time he happened to think of Gwrach.

"Mayhap she was able to cast a spell on ye treasure room door so that it opened without ye key," Syglinde suggested as they started back down the tower stairs.

"It's a thought," Shandy replied courteously. "And you say King Sfyn has never lent anybody the key before?"

"Why should he?" said Torchyld. "There be nothing inside that belongeth to any save only him and me. He begrudgeth me not, sin he knoweth full well I have e'en greater store of wealth than he. When Syggie and I move out, I shall leave some for him, for it be not meet that his liege be richer than he. This he knoweth though we have ne'er spoke of it, I not being one to vaunt my munificence and he not the sort to go around with his hand held out like some people I could mention."

"Very commendable," said Peter. "So to the best of your knowledge, you and he are the only ones who've had legitimate access to the strong room since you brought home the wyvern's hoard."

"Aye."

"When King Sfyn opened the door that other time, did it squeak?"

"Aye, it squeaked."

"You're positive?"

"In sooth, it did. A strong room door be supposed to squeak. That squeak be a vital link in ye castle's security. Gin any try to enter without Great-uncle Sfyn's leave, ye squeaking would be heard in ye sentry room above, and ye guard alerted. Then would ye miscreant be apprehended as soon as he set foot on ye step, and hurled back into ye dungeon, there to await ye king's displeasure. 'Tis a simple but foolproof system."

"Provided the door squeaked," Peter reminded him. "Didn't you notice when we opened it a little while ago that the door didn't make any sound at all?"

"Nay, I was noticing ye gleam of ye torchlight on Syglinde's hair, and thinking how much richer be that gold than all ye wyvern's hoard."

"And I was noticing ye little golden hairs on my Torchy's brawny arm, and ye strength of his hand as he tried to get ye key into ye lock wrong side up, and wondering if—I will not tell ye what I was wondering," Syglinde finished with a shy and secret smile.

"Well, if you care to return to the strong room, you'll find the lock and the hinges have all been lathered with eel fat to stop the squeaks. I presume that must have been done sometime during your absence these past few days."

"Aye, and that was when my gold and jewels were stolen. And ye hawk bell that was supposed to throw ye guilt on me gin it were discovered, I ween."

"I ween you've hit the nail on the head," Peter agreed. "Well, I don't suppose this is the optimum time to extract any information from your relatives, with a wedding and a funeral running neck-and-neck, but I might as well get on back to the great hall and see what I can scare up."

"And we must in sooth go back to ye strong room and choose wedding presents for Immie and Gwennie and ye others. And e'en for their lovesick swains." Syglinde couldn't stay serious for long, not with her own wedding on the docket, too. "And ye, Torchy darling, must choose one for me."

"Be not ye hand of an honest knight gift enough for ye, greedy wench?"

Laughing and teasing, the pair of them ran off. Peter, after a few wrong turns, found his way back to the great hall.

There, all was bustle and merriment, with Aunt Edelgysa bossing the job and everybody scurrying around getting in everybody else's way. The young ladies and their attendant lords had gone out into the fields around the castle and picked armloads of wildflowers. Now they were strewing some of these among clean rushes on the floor, or hanging great bunches of them from hooks on the wall. Their arrangements mightn't have passed muster with Grace Porble, head horticultural honcho of the Balaclava Junction Garden Club, but the effect was not without charm.

King Sfyn was up on the throne enjoying a nap in the midst of the hubbub. Dan Stott wasn't around. Somebody said he'd gone out to the pigpens with Prince Edbert, who took a keen personal interest in the royal livestock. The archdruid was down in the kitchens supervising the manufacture of a kettleful of soap. "We be all going to get baths for wedding presents," Hayward told Peter excitedly.

Shandy said that was nice, and went over to Prince Edwy, who wasn't doing anything but staring into space over the top of a flagon.

"Hail, prince," he said.

"Hail, bard," Edwy answered listlessly. "Have a drink."

"Not just now, thanks. I expect we'll all be toasting the happy couples in a while."

"Huh. Gin they but wotted what I wot." Prince Edwy swirled the ale around in his flagon, and scowled at the tiny whirlpool he'd created.

"What wot you, if I've phrased the question correctly?"

"Art not a married man thyself, bard?"

"Yes, I am. Quite happily married, in fact."

"And why happily? Because ye be here and she be elsewhere. Full many a flagon have I quaffed to some absent lord whilst I be enjoying his lady in his own castle. Belike some roving lord be quaffing now to ye, bard."

"I hardly think it likely."

Prince Edwy only smiled a wry smile, and emptied his flagon. Shandy shifted the tack slightly.

"You enjoy the roving life, I gather?"

" 'Tis the only life for a man, bard. Look at me, still in my prime, burning to go out and slay me another dragon—"

"And rescue another princess?"

"Gadzooks, have I not rescued one princess too many already? In course, were I to rescue a married princess with an absent lord—aye me, for ye open road and a mettlesome steed beneath me!"

"But you're second in line to the throne now, Prince Edwy. If anything should happen to Prince Dagobert—"

"Say not so, bard. E'en think it not. 'Tis a nightmare that haunteth me like a headless ghoul, that I might one day have to sit on ye throne and nevermore be free to rove. Not that I be free now. Alack and welladay. Where ye hell be all ye minions?"

Edwy was speaking the truth, Shandy decided. "Then you must be particularly concerned with keeping your father alive as long as possible," he observed.

"Aye, verily, that be I."

"Then perhaps you can tell me something I've been wondering about. Who stood guard over the king those nights the griffin wasn't available? Sir Torchyld tells me Ffyffnyr's the official royal watchdog."

Prince Edwy snorted. "Aye, I can tell ye. Edelgysa made me do it. Not that I minded, ye ken. Fond of ye old man and all that. It be just that acting as substitute for a griffin don't seem quite ye thing for a prince of ye blood. Nor care I much for sleeping in drafty doorways."

"Were you able to sleep all right? No—er—alarums and excursions?"

"Nay, 'twas peaceful enow. Old Dwydd mixed up some kind of muck that would enable me to sleep soundly, yet awaken instantly at ye merest sniff of danger. Seemed to work. At least nobody got assassinated or anything."

"That would appear to be conclusive proof, certainly. Let's see, you'd have been on guard duty for the past three nights."

Prince Edwy stared at Peter owlishly, did some complicated mental arithmetic, then nodded. "Aye. Last night, ye night before, and ye night before that."

"And you drank this potion each of the three nights, right? Who gave it to you? Dwydd herself?"

"Nay, Edelgysa brought it. I told her she might send it by Lady Megan to save herself ye labor, but she heeded me not."

"Her wifely devotion knows no bounds, eh?"

"Would that it did," said Edwy bitterly. "She e'en stood watching whilst I drank."

"Why, didn't you want to?"

"Nay, 'twas vile stuff. I protested that an old campaigner needeth no potion to sleep and wake as need ariseth, but she heeded me not. She avowed I would but fall into a drunken stupor and snore like a pig whilst enemies carried my father ye king off bodily."

"I see. She wanted to make sure you'd wake up. So what happened after you drank the potion?"

"I went to sleep."

"For how long?"

"Until I woke. Marry, bard, ye ask ridiculous questions."

"I meant, at what time did you wake? Was it before cockcrow?"

"Nay, ye sun was already climbing ye heavens and my father was bellowing for his morning ale. 'Twas his hullabaloo that roused me."

"Do tell. And this happened each time your wife gave you the potion?"

"Aye, that it did."

"Was this consistent with your usual pattern? That is, do you normally sleep as late as your father?"

"Nay, I be up with ye birds, doing mine exercises on ye bath mat. A prince must keep fit, gin he belike find ye chance to some day go another geste. Ho, carle, ye alepot!"

"At least I expect you'll get to lead the hawking expeditions from now on," Peter observed.

"Hawking, forsooth, I be but ye hunted rabbit, and yonder screameth ye great gyrfalcon."

Prince Edwy scowled over at Princess Edelgysa, who was berating her prospective son-in-law for not hanging a bouquet to suit her. "Mine only hope be that Prince Dagobert findeth himself a wife who be a bigger shrew than mine. Gin she be outyelled, perchance Edelgysa will go home to her mother and I be forced by family duties to remain in Sfynfford."

"Speaking of wives," said Peter, "I understand your son Owain had—er—hopes of Lady Syglinde."

"Aye, belike, but his mother desireth a princess for him. Ye richest princess in all ye land. Nothing be too good for her son."

"Owain's your son, too, isn't he?"

"I doubt not. Edelgysa be a virtuous woman, gin it come to that. Ye wilst not catch her shoving her husband off on ye gesting trail so she can entertain visiting lords." He took another gloomy pull at his flagon. "Too much virtue be a tiresome thing, bard."

"I suppose it could be, under certain circumstances," Shandy was forced to agree. "Er—let's get back to hawking. I'm still confused about what happened yesterday. As I understand it, Prince Edmyr was riding out in front. All by himself, was he? How close were you to him?"

"Two horse-lengths, thereabout."

"And Princess Edelgysa was beside you?"

"She was. Her palfrey kept snapping at my foot."

"Then in fact she was not precisely beside, but a little behind. Could you see her, or would you have had to turn your head?"

"Nay, I turned not my head. I see enow of Edelgysa without trying."

"You were looking straight ahead, were you? At Prince Edmyr?"

"Nay, I was half asleep, gin ye crave ye truth. I knew my steed would follow ye leader. He be a trusty friend who hath carried me safe o'er many a mile whilst I drowsed in ye saddle, dreaming of ye glad old days when he and I roved wild and free."

"Noble of him. Do you recall who else was close to you?"

"That I can, bard. Nobody. See ye, none list to ride anear Edelgysa. She layeth too free about her with her whip."

"You mean she beats her horse?"

"She beats whate'er cometh in her way. She liketh fine to whip ye heads of flowers as she rideth, or to flick ye flies off ye horses. She can kill a fly with one flick at full gallop without touching ye hide of ye horse."

"You don't say. That's quite a skill. She uses a long whip, I suppose."

"Nay, 'tis but a dainty thing, fit for a woman's hand. 'Twas her skill at flicking flies that made me think I loved her. Ah, woe to ye fool who fell for a fleetly flailing fly-flicker."

Edwy burst into tears and laid his head on the banqueting table. Seconds later, he was out like a light. So much for that interview.

Shandy wished he could corner Princess Edelgysa and ask a few pointed questions about that potion she'd been dosing her husband with, but there'd be no chance of getting her attention now. She was buzzing around like a wroth hornet, although her mood appeared to be relatively amiable at the moment. Her daughter, Princess Aloisa, was showing off one of the garments from her trousseau.

"She how fine and lustrous ye thread," she was boasting. " 'Tis of my mother's spinning. None other can spin so well as Princess Edelgysa. Be that not so, Mother?"

"It be," Edelgysa replied modestly. "I be without peer at ye spindle. There be no threads, be they woolen or flax, stronger nor smoother than mine in all ye kingdom."

"You don't say," Shandy murmured. He strolled over to Prince Dagobert, who was sitting by himself in a corner looking glum.

"Care to take a little canter, Your Highness?"

Dagobert gazed up at him with red-rimmed eyes. "A canter like ye one my father took?"

"Not like that, no. I simply want you to help me look for something."

As Peter had suspected, the young crown prince had brains. Dagobert got up and led the way out to the stables without further comment. It was a revelation to see how many horses King Sfyn possessed, and how handsomely they were kept. Despite the equine plurality, the ostlers offered Peter a mule they evidently kept for visiting clergy. He accepted without any fuss. Peter liked mules. Dagobert chose a sturdy roan, not the horse he'd been riding earlier, and they were off.

"I want to cover as exactly as possible the terrain you were on when your father fell," Peter explained. "Do you think you can recall the spot?"

"Could I e'er forget?"

"Sorry, that was stupid of me. Let me ask you this, if I may. I understand it's your Aunt Edelgysa's habit to carry a small riding whip that she constantly flicks at flowers and insects as she rides?"

"Aye, and at nephews and nieces and lords and ladies-in-waiting, gin she taketh a notion. We all strive to ride clear of Aunt Edelgysa and her little whip."

"Then tell me, was your aunt using the whip as freely as usual today?"

The question surprised Dagobert. "I—let me bethink myself."

"By all means. Bethink as hard as you like. It's important."

"She had it in her hand as she rode," Dagobert said slowly. "That I be sure of. But—nay, bard, she struck her palfrey to make it run when my father's horse broke into a gallop, but otherwise she used it not. How did ye divine that?"

"I have my methods. Now think again. You say she hit her palfrey when your father's horse started to run. Does that mean just before, just after, or at precisely the same moment?"

Dagobert pondered a moment, then gasped. " 'Twas before. Had it been afterward I might well not have noticed, for mine own mount caught ye fever of ye chase and bolted after ye lead horse. I was not ready, and had my hands full reining him in."

"Why weren't you ready?"

"We ne'er gallop o'er that patch of ground. It be a steep hillside, ye ken, and hillocky. I wondered what madness had o'ertaken my father on a sudden."

"But you say your aunt whipped up her horse first."

"Aye, she did. And 'twas an odd way she did it. I mind me now. She first hit her mount one smart clip on ye rump, then she leaned forward and raised her arm as if to strike ye head. I saw not ye lash, but I recall well ye raised arm and ye forward lunge. Bard Pete, this maketh no sense. It be not ye done thing to override ye master of ye hunt. Aunt Edelgysa knoweth well ye rule, and she be hottest of all ye court to see everything done according to protocol. Yet one whippeth not a horse by accident. She must have meant to do what she did."

"Oh yes," said Peter, "I have no doubt whatever your aunt meant to do exactly what she did. Ah, I think I see what I was looking for. Just a moment."

He climbed down from his mule, scrambled among the nettles for a moment, and came up with stung legs and a long strand of expertly spun black linen thread.

"All right, Dagobert. We can go home now."

CHAPTER 18

Not every man could contrive to look majestic with a three days' sprouting of gray whiskers on his face, but Daniel Stott, temporary assistant archdruid to the court of King Sfyn, managed it without even trying. Marrying off seven couples at a time was no big deal to a man who'd presided over the nuptial rites of whole herds of cows, whole flocks of sheep, whole gaggles of geese, and even one whole muster of peacocks. Dan had Tim stand at his right side wearing a wreath of mistletoe and carrying his golden sickle. The trappings might not have been appropriate, but they certainly added a touch of class.

Peter was at Dan's left side with a rose behind his ear and his harp at the ready. The Welsh taste for music not yet being developed to the high state it would attain in centuries to come, Peter did not scruple to render his own version of "I Love You Truly" as the brides tripped gaily in through one door and the bridegrooms stamped nervously through another, all scrubbed with fresh-made eel fat soap and wearing spanking clean garments in bright array.

Six of the brides were loaded down with the wedding gifts their wooers had brought, along with presents from King Sfyn and Sir Torchyld, and various other bits and pieces. Lady Syglinde contented herself with one magnificent golden bracelet that was the king's gift, and a ruby necklace from the wyvern's hoard. Nevertheless, she outshone the rest as the moon outshines a candle flame.

Lord Ysgard's boys appeared quite content with their flames. Privately they'd decided a wife like Lady Syglinde would take a lot of living up to; whereas Immie, Gwennie, Guinnie, Gwladdie, Allie, and Bloddie were cozy, cuddly girls who could keep track of where a fellow had parked his codpiece when he was going out to battle, and have a hot meal waiting for him when he got back.

All in all, it was a lovely wedding. At the marriage feast afterward, Peter sang, "Drink to Me Only with Thine Eyes." His hearers found that a hilarious notion as they sent the drinking horn splashing merrily around the table. Everybody got at least mildly sloshed except Torchyld and Syglinde. Those two just sat holding hands and drinking to each other only with their eyes.

Peter caught Princess Edelgysa watching the pair narrowly, her lips tight. The rest of the parents, even Princess Aldora despite her recent bereavement, were waxing mirthful with their daughters and their just-gained sons, consoling each other with reminders that Ysgard wasn't all that far away and they'd be tottling back and forth for picnics, joustings, may-pole-dancings, hangings, and such festivities.

Come morning, there would be the funeral of Prince Edmyr, then the funeral feast. Afterward, brides and bridegrooms would ride off to Ysgard, accompanied by sundry relatives, attendants, and plump serving maids to gladden the hearts of the boys back home. Sir Torchyld and his new-made lady would stay with King Sfyn.

What Peter, Tim, and Dan would do had not yet been decided. Peter was cherishing a hope that the completion of these various ceremonies would somehow mark the grand finale of their unsought adventure. In the meantime, however, he still had a duty to perform. It was not going to be a happy one. He hadn't the heart to hurl his bombshell into the midst of the wedding festivities, but he'd be taking an awful risk if he put if off much longer.

Dagobert was probably safe enough. The crown prince knew the situation now, and he was a clever lad. He'd make a good king. Better than Torchyld, most likely. Torchyld was still too guileless. He'd be a good husband, a good father, a good lord of the manor, and a damned good man in a dustup, but he did have a lot to learn about enchantments.

Speaking of which, Peter hadn't seen Dwydd around. Had he really succeeded in intimidating her, or was she only lying low hatching up fresh perfidy? Nobody'd missed the resident hag, at any rate. The revelry was beginning to break up. Bridegrooms were nudging brides and whispering urgent suggestions into their ears. Brides were flouncing and blushing and nodding their heads. Princess Aldora, whose stock of good humor must be wearing thin by now, rose to address the king.

"My liege, this hath been a full day and a merry one. Wouldst now give leave for these happy couples to repair unto their nuptial chambers and rest themselves for ye morrow?"

"That be what they're going for?" Owain murmured archly.

His remark set off the usual spate of wedding-night jokes, many of which were still being used, Peter was interested to note, back—or would it be forward—in Balaclava County. The weary chestnuts would no doubt get exported to alien planets along with the space colonies of the future, if they weren't already being rehashed in flying saucers throughout the galaxy. Perhaps they'd first been uttered by the serpent as Adam and Eve headed for the shrubbery of Eden, shedding fig leaves en route.

Maybe King Sfyn was tired of the jokes, too, or maybe he knew the newlyweds would sneak off anyway. He graciously gave them permission to retire. Now that the subject had come up, he thought he'd turn in early, himself. It would be nice to have old Ffyff guarding the door again.

King and griffin hied themselves bedward. Lords, ladies, and chamberlains of the bedchamber started grabbing the bouquets down from the walls. The flowers were wilted by now, but still serviceable for strewing under the footsteps of the bridal couples, where they'd only get stepped on anyway.

Torchyld and Syglinde stayed apart from the skylarking; not by absenting themselves from the rest, but simply by being oblivious of anyone but each other. That bothered Peter. He took it upon himself to tag along and make a thorough search of their bedchamber. Torchyld noticed at last that he and his bride were not alone, and took umbrage.

"Do ye leave quietly, bard, or do I assist ye?"

"Don't get into a swivet," said Peter. "I'll go in a minute. I

just want to make damned sure there's nothing in your bed
that shouldn't be here."

Syglinde laughed. "Such as what? Prince Owain?"

"Such as a venomous snake or a poisoned thorn, since you
ask. I hate to put a damper on the fun, kids, but it would be a
shame to have your honeymoon end before it ever got started.
How'd you feel, Torchyld, if it was your wife instead of yourself
who got killed by mistake?"

"Arrgh!"

"But if Torchy were to die, think ye I would let myself go on
living?" Syglinde sobbed from the depths of the massive bo-
som to which she was being desperately clutched. "Why speak
ye these dreadful utterings, Bard Pete? Tonight, all should be
joy and love."

"All will be, if you'll simply let me exercise a few rudimen-
tary precautions. By tomorrow, your trouble will be over. I
promise."

Because tonight he, Peter Shandy, was going to camp on a
certain doorstep and make damned sure the person inside
didn't take a notion to sleepwalk. Maybe he'd have been wiser
to blow the whistle sooner, but how far would that have got
him? His case was tenuous, to say the least, and he was dealing
here not with knaves and churls, but with a royal family that
had its own headsman on the payroll. Guile and diplomacy
were needed. He borrowed Lady Syglinde's sharp little knife,
left the newlyweds to their well-deserved *digrifwch,* and cleared
out.

Guard duty was no great chore. Peter's only trouble lay in
staying awake. To beguile the hours, he whittled at those three
slender wands he'd been carrying with him ever since the
morning he'd escaped from Gwrach's cave. After he'd got
them smoothed to his liking, he added small bedizenments. At
last, when cocks began to crow and the sun to do their raucous
bidding, he decided it was safe to assume his quarry wouldn't
try anything funny now, and betook himself to the kitchen.
There he found a minion astir, made known his requirement,
and got what he'd gone for, along with a pledge of silence. At

last he went along to the chapel, where Prince Edmyr lay in solitary state with guttered candles at his head and feet.

Normally, no doubt, there would have been an honor guard with members of the family mourning in shifts beside the body. Last night's multiple wedding had made it necessary to cancel the vigil. That was fine as far as Peter was concerned, and Edmyr didn't appear to be minding. He performed a few experiments, nodded to himself when he'd got the hang of what he wanted to do, carefully arranged the little bundle he'd brought from the kitchen under the heavy purple pall that covered Prince Edmyr's bier, and went to break his fast.

King Sfyn and Ffyffnyr were the first ones down this morning. It was a heartening sight to watch them sharing a trencherful of boiled eels in comradely silence. Shandy took a manchet of bread and was munching on it when Dan Stott and Timothy Ames entered the banqueting hall, anxious to get the obsequies over with and hoping to God they wouldn't have to perform any more solemn druidic rites until they could get hold of a real druid and get some idea of what in fact a druidic rite was.

Then came Prince Edwy and Prince Edbert, both of them red-eyed and morose from the combined aftereffects of the wedding carouse and the prospect of having to bury their elder brother. Their ladies, they explained, were still upstairs packing folderols for their daughters to take to Ysgard. As for the brides and bridegrooms, they didn't appear until after King Sfyn had sent up a posse of ladies-in-waiting with terse messages about the fun's being over and the solemnities about to start. At last they straggled in, herded by the three elder princesses, also red-eyed but far from morose and displaying well-whetted appetites.

Sir Torchyld and Lady Syglinde were the very last ones down, looking so radiant that Princess Edelgysa made a caustic remark about people who didn't know enough to put on sober faces for sad occasions.

"I was sober enow when my Torchyld went to kill ye wyvern and I wist not gin he would e'er return," Syglinde retorted. "I wept when he was falsely reviled by those who also should have known better for stealing Ffyffnyr, and when I was cruelly rapt from his side by ye evil wiles of Dwydd. None mourned for me then. Now that my love and I be together as man and wife, I find it hard to mourn for anyone else. But I do feel for Princess Aldora and Gwennie and Immie, and most of all for Prince Dagobert."

She went over and gave the widow a hug and a kiss. "When we have our own manor, ye will come and stay with us, and tell us about your beautiful grandchildren. 'Tis some comfort, belike, that when one life is over, another beginneth. We must next find a wife for Dagobert."

"I expect I'll have abundance of wives to choose from, once ye word goeth around that I be now heir to ye throne," said the crown prince cynically. "Grandfather, a boon. Now that we be all assembled and our fast broken, may we not get on with ye funeral rites? My sisters and cousins and their husbands have yet a long journey to travel. And I, I fear, have a longer and a wearier."

"Being king hath its good side as well as its bad," said his royal grandsire kindly. "Be of cheer, Dagobert."

"Aye, Dagobert, be of cheer," echoed Owain with a sneer in his voice. "Cry we all, 'Long live ye king,' and so mote it be."

"We hae talked enough," cried Princess Edelgysa. "An it please Your Majesty, let us now repair to ye chapel for ye solemn rites, and thence to ye burial. Be ye archdruid ready?"

"As ready as I'm ever going to be," said Tim. "Assistant Archdruid Dan Stott will deliver the eulogy, followed by the head bard singing 'Abide with Me' with harp accompaniment. You remember the words, Pete?"

"Certainly." Peter had a phenomenal memory for verse. "I thought maybe I'd recite 'The Cremation of Sam McGee' for an encore. Or do you think they'd prefer the one about Mad Carew?"

"Let's play it by ear." Tim sounded ridiculously pleased with himself. "All set, everybody? Let's go wash off the eel grease and buckle down to work. You folks go first and grab your seats, then the boys and I will enter in solemn procession. See you in church. Cripes, I'm really perking today."

"Well, simmer down," Peter told him *sotto voce.* "We've got some serious business on hand here. Listen, this is what we do after Dan finishes the eulogy."

He explained. Stott nodded. "An excellent plan, friend Pete. And you wish Tim and myself to be on the *qui vive* for signs of undue agitation among the congregants."

"I expect they'll all be pretty agitated. You just stand by to grab the one who tries to run."

They marched into the chapel, Peter strumming "We shall meet but we shall miss him" as reverently as he could manage, and Dan, who had a fine bass voice with a range of almost half an octave, droning a sort of bagpipe accompaniment. Tim, who couldn't have carried a tune in a basket, confined himself to lifting his sickle now and then in some intricate gesticulations that didn't mean anything but seemed to impress the congregation. They marched twice around the bier, then took up strategic positions according to their prearranged plan.

Daniel Stott, who could make even a page of hog statistics sound impressive, recited several of the more affecting verses from sympathy cards received at the time of his first wife Elizabeth's demise. Then he launched into a stirring eulogy, touching on Prince Edmyr's prowess in the hawking field, his lofty bearing and premonarchical mien, on the loss to his family and to the realm occasioned by his demise, and on a number of other things that might or might not have any particular relevance to the deceased. The eulogy was well constructed, eloquently delivered, and probably not more inanely inappropriate than most. When Dan showed symptoms of running down, Peter stepped forward.

"And now comes the time for each person here to pay his or her last respects to our departed crown prince. Led by your monarch, will you all rise and walk slowly past the bier?"

"Nay!" Old Dwydd had come out of hiding, all set to do battle. "It be unlucky to bestir ye atmosphere around ye dead, lest his ghost come to afright us."

"His ghost will not walk in this holy place," said Peter sternly, "unless there be someone among you who is guilty of having caused his death. No innocent person need fear to perform this rite. To refuse in the presence of the king and the archdruid, would constitute a confession of guilt. Now rise and pass along, as the archdruid directs. Slowly and reverently, please."

After that, nobody would have dared hang back. Tim stood like a French gendarme, directing traffic past the bier while Peter made indeterminate noises on the harp strings. One by one, the family walked over to Prince Edmyr's corpse and around the bier. Peter watched narrowly. At the critical moment, praying his aim was true, he fitted one of the improvised arrows he'd worked on during the night to a string of his harp, drew back the string as far as he could, and fired.

Bull's-eye! The pig's bladder he'd filled in the kitchen and hidden under the cerecloth burst with an audible pop, spraying blood all over the skirt of Princess Edelgysa.

"Ooh!" The shriek went up all through the chapel. Edelgysa herself reared like a startled mare, her face as white as her robe.

Princess Aldora and Prince Dagobert flew at her. "Wicked woman! 'Twas ye who killed our loved one!"

"Ye lie," she shrieked back. "I ne'er laid hand on him."

Peter stepped forward and surreptitiously reclaimed his arrow. "You didn't have to touch him. That little whip you wield so handily, as everyone here can testify, did the job for you."

"Impossible," screamed Dwydd. "Her whip be but a toy, and she was two horse-lengths away from ye prince. I was there. I saw."

"Prince Dagobert was there, also," said Peter. "He saw Princess Edelgysa hit up her horse and swing her whip forward just before Prince Edmyr fell. Yesterday afternoon, Prince Dagobert and I found the heavy black thread she'd used to lengthen out the whip lash and kept hidden in her hand as she rode. That was why she hadn't been using her whip as usual during the ride. She'd weighted the end of the thread with a silver hawk bell. She may have meant to hit the horse and make it bolt. Instead, the bell struck Prince Edmyr at the base of his skull, probably stunning him momentarily and causing him to lose control of his mount, which broke into a gallop, stumbled,

and threw him with fatal results, as you know. Unfortunately
for her plan, the bell broke through the thread and remained
caught in Prince Edmyr's hood, where it was found yesterday
in your presence. She'd stolen the bell from the king's treasure
room, along with a number of more valuable items."

"She robbed ye king?" That seemed to horrify the congregation far more than the idea of her having caused Prince
Edmyr's death. Naturally enough, perhaps, in this era when
heirs to thrones were always sitting targets for assassination.

"Ye lie, bard," shouted Prince Owain, who must have realized whom she'd done it for. "How could my mother get into
ye strong room? It be aye locked, and ye king keepeth ye key."

"She drugged him. Dwydd mixed her a potion to drug both
King Sfyn and your father, who was keeping guard during
Ffyffnyr's enforced absence. They slept so soundly that she
was able to sneak in and steal the key, then put it back later
without getting caught. Prince Edwy has already testified that
his wife persuaded him to drink such a draft, under the pretext
that it would give him a good night's rest, but cause him to
wake instantly if anyone tried to get at the king."

"And how, prithee, did she manage to drug my grandfather?"

The old king looked up at his too-handsome grandson.
"Easy enow, I ween. Thy mother came to me all pitying and
condoled with me on ye loss of Ffyffnyr. Then gave she me a
magic potion to quaff. She said it might send me a soothsayer's
dream to show me what had become of Ffyff. It only made me
dream of lizards crawling up inside my vizard. That would
have been her wicked fingers, I doubt not, brushing o'er me to
get at ye key."

"I be falsely accused," cried Princess Edelgysa. She had
nerve, at any rate. "What be these things he claimeth I took
from ye strong room? How could it be known what be missing
from those many eel baskets heaped high with treasure?"

"The fact that you know about the eel baskets might be a
point against you, but we don't need it," said Peter. "To answer your question, we know what you took because the
amount of treasure now in the baskets doesn't tally with the

record made at the time the wyvern's hoard was locked away. Would you care to give us an itemized account, Lady Syglinde?"

Sir Torchyld's new bride, blushing importantly, fiddled with her slates as all good treasurers do with their account books, then read off the missing items. "And ye necklace with stones like dewdrops be ye same she weareth now, albeit it be too dressy for a funeral," she finished. " 'Tis ye one I wanted Torchy to give me for our wedding, so I know."

Princess Gwynedd caught her breath. "I did wonder where Edelgysa got so rare a jewel on a sudden," she said in a kind of stifled shriek. "She sought to persuade me 'twas from her great-aunt Maud's estate."

Princess Aldora roused herself from her paroxysms of grief long enough to snort; a regal and ladylike snort, to be sure, but nonetheless a snort. "Her great-aunt Maud's estate, forsooth! Maud had scarce a robe to cover her back, let alone fine jewels for her neck. 'Twas she who ran away with a mad wizard and became his—By my halidom, I see all now. 'Tis Dwydd! Bethink ye, Gwynedd, what ye traveling minstrel told us, that ye wizard had died of his own poison and Maud was seeking employ as a resident hag. 'Twas shortly after that Edelgysa found Dwydd ye post here with Papa Sfyn. Behold, she hath a look of Edelgysa around ye eyes. So, Maud, 'twas ye who abetted thy niece in her wicked designs to obtain ye throne for her spoiled brat Owain."

"She forced me," Dwydd quavered. "I could do no other."

"There, she sweareth! Confess, Edelgysa, all be revealed. Ye blood hath told, in more ways than one."

Everybody was either gaping at Dwydd or shuddering at the pool of blood under the bier. Seeing their attention withdrawn from her, Princess Edelgysa leaped for the door. Tim, who'd been watching for such a move, tried to stop her. She shoved him aside with the strength of desperation, and kept going. Dan Stott then moved to block her way, but she gave him a savage left hook in the belly and left him gasping. Peter almost reached her, but she slammed the heavy chapel door in his face and lowered the bar, penning them all inside.

It took a fair amount of pounding and hollering before some minion happened to hear and came to let them out. By then, Princess Edelgysa had reached the stables.

"Raise ye drawbridge," ordered King Sfyn.

That didn't stop Edelgysa. She galloped headlong toward the moat, frantically whipping up her horse for the impossible jump. The heavy beast, bred to carry armored knights, could never have made it. He caught his foot in a basket of fresh-caught eels and stumbled, shooting Princess Edelgysa headlong into the soft mud at the bottom. Torchyld, Prince Dagobert, Prince Owain, Prince Edwy, Prince Edbert, Prince Gelert, and Prince Gaheris all jumped in after her, stirring up the silt and making it impossible for any of them to see anything under the water. By the time they'd groped their way to her, Princess Edelgysa was dead.

"Mayhap 'twas all for ye best," said Syglinde, wiping mud off Torchyld's face. " 'Twould have been an unseemly execution, with her bossing ye headsman around and complaining about ye dullness of ye ax."

Prince Owain threw Torchyld's bride a remarkably Aunt-Maudish look, then strode over and knelt before the king.

"Sire, a boon. Grant me permission to go on a geste. To stay here now would be intolerable to me."

"Aye, grandson, go and prosper. Belike ye will find a wyvern to slay."

"Belike he will find a rich widow to cozen," Dagobert murmured.

Prince Edwy went over to clap his son on the shoulder. "Great idea, Owain. Shake ye dust of ye court from ye feet and get out among ye fearsome dragons and ill-tempered knights errant. Nothing like a spot of slashing and slaying to take a young prince's mind off his troubles."

He in turn hurled himself at King Sfyn's feet. "Father, I crave pardon for having been ye instrument of bringing this dire misfortune upon our house. Had I but wist what Edelgysa was really like, I'd have let ye dragon keep her in ye first place. Prithee grant me also leave to erase this stain from our escutcheon by myself going back to ye gesting trail."

"Aye, son," said the old king, "gin ye swear a solemn oath to refrain from rescuing any more princesses. God speed ye both. Ho, gravediggers. Dig an extra hole and let us get on with ye obsequies."

CHAPTER 19

It was a strange feeling, to have watched the planting of a murderess and a murderee side by side in the same burying ground, Peter thought, but at least it was over now. Everything seemed to be over: all the young lovers married, Prince Edwy and Prince Owain off on their geste, the wicked hag gone nobody knew where, the red griffin and the old king happily reunited. Surely this mad fairy tale ought to be coming to an end for himself and his friends, too. Peter felt a profound reluctance to reenter the castle. He turned aside and began examining the exterior architecture, which in fact he'd had little opportunity to do thus far.

Sir Torchyld noticed, and came over to join him, looking rather naked without Syglinde glued to his side. She had gone to comfort Princess Aldora, whose own daughters were too busy getting ready for their upcoming trip to Ysgard to notice their mother's grief.

"Bard Pete," said the knight, "I crave to ask by what means ye sent ye feathered shaft through ye pig's bladder full of chicken blood when ye were standing a full three lance-lengths from my uncle's bier."

"Oh, you noticed, did you?"

"Aye, and marveled. 'Twould have been nigh impossible e'en for me to throw so flimsy a wand hard enough to pierce ye cerecloth and ye bladder from such a distance. 'Twas necromancy, I misdoubt."

"Not at all," Peter assured him. "Simply an application of the principle of propulsion. Let me demonstrate. Here's another stick like the one I shot. They're called arrows, for your information."

"Arrows. 'Tis a pretty name, but a paltry weapon."

"Not when shot with force. You see, what I did was this."

Peter set his harp to his shoulder, fitted the nock of his makeshift arrow to a taut harp string, and pulled back on it. The harp's frame was a flimsy thing of supple wood, probably manufactured by Dwydd herself for the sole purpose of turning Torchyld into a bard and probably never really meant to be played. It bowed in an reasonably satisfactory manner, and Peter let go. The arrow shot through the air and pierced the basket of eels that was still sitting beside the moat.

"There, you see how it's done. You don't need a harp, of course. You'd be better off with a plain stave of wood—yew, I believe, is an excellent choice—about as long as the span of your outstretched arms. This would be called a bow, since it gets bowed into an arc when you pull on the bowstring, which is attached to the ends much as the strings are attached to this harp. See what I mean?"

Peter borrowed Torchyld's dagger to cut a long, slender sapling, notch it at both ends, and string it with the long thread he'd been carrying as evidence of Princess Edelgysa's perfidy. "This is very rough, of course. You'd skin off the bark, flatten the stave to make it more flexible, and perhaps wrap a piece of leather around the center to give yourself a firm handhold. There are any number of ways you could improve the design, and I'm sure you'll find them, since you and your countrymen are destined to give the longbow to Western civilization."

"Ye hell we be. Such a splendid weapon, we shall keep to ourselves. A bow, ye say, and an arrow." Torchyld flexed the sapling in wonderment. " 'Tis a wonder, Bard Pete. A bowman would need more than one arrow, meseems. In ye heat of battle, he could not go out among ye enemy to pick them up once they be shotten."

"Good point," said Peter. "I'm sure you'll have the bugs worked out in no time. Well, Torchyld, I expect this is as good a time as any to say good-bye."

"Bard Pete, ye cannot leave us now. Ye peril be past and 'tis time for merrymaking. Also, I need ye to help Syggie and me choose an auspicious place to build our house."

"You'll know the place when you come to it, Torchyld. As for my friends and myself, I'm afraid we really have to push on. You see, we have a geste of our own. We were just setting out on it, as a matter of fact, when we ran into you and—er—things took their course."

"Aye, so they did, and with fortunate outcome for me, whenas I foresaw naught but misery. Ye have sworn a solemn oath to perform this geste?"

"M'well, yes, I suppose you could say that." Letting the university pay for his plane ticket must constitute a moderately firm commitment, Peter thought.

"Then no word of mine can stay ye. But I shall miss ye, Bard Pete, ye and ye revered though somewhat peculiar archdruid and ye honorable Dan, who can eat even Ffyff under ye table. I feel a bond betwixt us, gin we be in some way brothers. Think ye we may one day meet again?"

"I'd bet my bottom dollar on it," Peter assured him. "Now I expect I'd better go round up the boys and get our little show on the road."

Not that he had the remotest idea where they were going; he only knew the time had come to go. Interestingly enough, his comrades must have got the same message. As he passed under the portcullis, he met both Tim and Dan coming toward him.

"Whither bound, mates?" he asked them.

"Hell," said Tim, "we were hoping you'd know. Dan and I just decided we couldn't stand the smell of rotten booze and eel grease any longer."

"That doesn't surprise me," said Peter. "I was coming in to see how you lads felt about pushing on. Have you made your farewells to King Sfyn and the rest of the crowd?"

"Sort of," said Tim. "There was such a mob of granddaughters around the old coot we're not sure he heard us, but what the hell? We figured if we hung around they'd think we were looking for presents and horses and whatnot, so we patted the griffin and cleared out."

"I concurred with Tim in this regard," said Dan. "It struck me that we had best go away with no more than we came with, although I did pack us a modest lunch from the leftovers on the banqueting table. Also, it might perhaps be deemed not out of order for you to keep the harp."

"Nothing doing," said Peter. "I'm going to hang my harp on a weeping willow tree and never, never play again. Oh, fare thee well for we must leave thee, do not let the parting grieve thee, and remember that ye best of friends must part. So long, Torchyld. Give our fondest regards to Lady Syglinde, and may all your troubles be little ones. Come on quick, boys, before he starts to cry again."

They waved a last good-bye to the no longer unfortunate young knight, crossed the drawbridge, and let the forest engulf them. Any path was the right path, according to Dan's reckoning. Apparently all they had to do was make themselves available and trust in fate to overtake them.

Fate didn't seem to be in the mood, however. Nothing came in their way except a couple of curious rabbits. They wandered along the leafy glades, missing their new friends but glad enough to be rid of the troubles that had beset them since they'd crossed the bridge of time. They simply kept going until they were tired, then found a pleasant little brook, sat down on the mossy bank beside it, and ate the manchets and cold fowl Dan had thought to bring along. Plain water from the brook tasted fine after all that thick, flat ale they'd had to drink, first at Lord Ysgard's and then at King Sfyn's.

After they'd finished, Peter remarked, "Since we don't appear to be in a rush to get anywhere, boys, I think I'll just shut my eyes for a few minutes, if you don't mind. I didn't get any sleep last night."

"Why not?" Tim murmured drowsily.

"I sat up keeping an eye on Princess Edelgysa. I was afraid she'd try to bump off Torchyld again. Not to mention Prince Dagobert and very likely her own husband as well. I don't think she was much impressed by my having found that hawk bell. She'd got away with killing Dilwyn. God knows how but it should have been easy enough—some muck Dwydd cooked up for her, I suppose—and she was cocky enough to think we'd never see through the stunt she pulled on Prince Edmyr."

"We might not have, had it not been for your keen powers of observation and deduction," said Dan Stott.

"Oh, I don't know. She was fairly blatant about it, really. The big problem was of course to stop her. Having got the bit in her teeth, she might have gone on till she'd wiped out the whole court."

"Like a dog killing sheep," Dan agreed. "Once they start, there is no stopping them, short of a bullet. Sad as it may be."

Dan fell to ruminating. Peter fell asleep. So, it may be conjectured, did Timothy Ames. Perhaps all those naps he'd shared with King Sfyn lately had left him more rested than the others, however. In any event, it was Tim who gave the alarm.

"Pete! Hey, Pete, wake up. I think I hear something."

"Ungh? Great Scott, I'll say you do? Dan! Dan, what does that sound like to you?"

"Eh? Oh." Daniel Stott barely stopped to ruminate before he performed the unaccustomed act of leaping to his feet. "My friends, I fear we are about to be again overtaken by the giant hogweed. I suggest we depart this place with all celerity."

"Cripes, yes," cried Tim, "but where to?"

"Across the brook, one might think. The water may impede the hogweed's progress."

"But the brook only sprang from a spring up yonder," Peter argued. "All the hogweed has to do is go around behind it and grow down the other side."

"Well, we damn well better spring somewhere fast," said Tim. "Here she comes."

And there it came, a rustling wall of fifteen-foot stalks, nodding dirty white umbels and flapping ugly gray-green leaves.

"This way," yelled Peter. "Let's try to outflank it."

Even as he shouted, however, the grotesque living wall bent itself into a horseshoe formation, throwing up wings on either side. As before, the hogweed was leaving them no choice.

They took the only direction open to them, the one in which the hogweed wanted them to go, and ran till they could go no farther. A solid rock cliff was blocking their way. Peter realized with despair that he recognized the locale. As the hogweed pressed in upon them, he pulled his companions with him back into the mouth of Gwrach's cave.

"Oh my God," Tim groaned. "Not this again."

"Afraid so," Peter grunted. "I just hope that old sow hasn't managed to pull herself together. You don't suppose we have any hope of finding our way through to the other end?"

"Gin ye will please to follow me, sires."

The glow was back. "Great Scott!" Peter exclaimed. "Is that you, Medrus?"

"At your service, noble sirs. Pray exercise due caution amongst ye falling stones. They be jarred loose by ye pressure of ye hogweed against ye mouth of ye cave. Gin ye will forgive ye presumption, I recommend full speed ahead."

"To where?" Peter demanded, even though it was plain to see that the crumbling roof gave them no choice except to go with the glow or stay and be buried alive. "Don't tell us Gwrach is back in business?"

"Nay, Bard Pete. Gwrach be destroyed."

"Then how come you've got your old job back?"

"I happened to be in ye vicinity and heard ye sound of pursuit. Hence I bethought me to come to ye rescue."

"All by yourself, eh?"

"I be trained to ye job, sire."

"So ye be. What happened to Lord Ysgard? Isn't he still with you?"

"Lord Ysgard be within," Medrus replied, flickering slightly. "Ye fact of ye matter be this, noble bard. As ye might have deemed, Gwrach accumulated a treasure of no inconsiderable magnitude by robbing her victims before she killed and ate them. Being, as ye wist, without employ or prospects, I sought to ingratiate myself with Lord Ysgard by apprising him of ye fact and suggesting he come to gain ye hoard under my guidance."

"Whom were you trying to ingratiate yourself with when you set that booby trap for Sir Torchyld on the battlements back at Castle Ysgard?" Peter demanded.

The glow remained steady this time. "With Dwydd, honored bard. Gin ye come now frae ye castle of King Sfyn, ye have

mayhap encountered a sorceress of that name. I wot not gin
she hath by now encompassed ye death of Sir Torchyld, but I
wist ere yet I met ye that Dwydd and my late employer Gwrach
of malodorous memory had entered into a conspiracy to destroy him. Methought sin Gwrach's plan had gone awry, I
might gain favor in Dwydd's eyne by acting in her stead. Thus
perchance could I avail myself of Dwydd's power over ye giant
hogweed, in my geste to obtain Gwrach's treasure. 'Twas but
an idle hope, methinks, but I could not afford to let ye chance
go by. A wight in my position needeth all ye help he can get."

"Regardless of whose expense he gets it at, eh?"

"I but followed ye examples of my former masters, noble
bard. Be an humble clerk supposed to ken better than his
betters?"

"Cripes," Tim remarked. "What do you want to bet this bird
reincarnates as a Philadelphia lawyer?"

"I should not be at all surprised," Dan Stott agreed. "But,
Medrus, why did you seek to engage Lord Ysgard in your
venture? Why not come alone and secure Gwrach's hoard
entirely to yourself?"

"Nay, noble assistant archdruid. Bethink ye, were a mere
clerk like me to show his face in any town beladen with gold
and gems, I should be clapt into prison as a thief and a rogue,
and tortured until ye magistrates wrung from me ye secret of
mine hoard. Gin I made Lord Ysgard his fortune through my
fealty, I might hope at least to get a steady job out of it. He
wisteth ye force of mine argument. Being himself somewhat
low in ye coffers, he agreed to ye geste, and here we be."

"Bully for you," said Peter. "Have you found the treasure
yet?"

"I had not to seek, sire. I wist already where it lay, having oft
been forced to light Gwrach her way whilst she added ye purse
of yet another luckless wight to her ill-got store. Picking her
teeth with his rib bone ye while, belike. 'Tis one of Lord
Ysgard's more amiable traits that he continueth not to make
loud sucking noises long after he hath broken his fast. Such
habits be more trying to ye nerves of ye upper servants than ye
aristocracy wotteth."

"I can well imagine," said Peter. "So where is Lord Ysgard, and where is this hoard of Gwrach's?"

"Yonder," said Medrus. "Observe ye large puddle, prithee."

"M'yes, very pretty. Who changed you back into a glow?"

Peter hadn't found much reason to trust Medrus during their earlier adventures, and he wasn't inclined to do so now. He thought the recharged glow was probably telling the truth about Gwrach's amassed treasure and why he'd persuaded Lord Ysgard to come after it with him, but he didn't at all care for the way Medrus was evading his questions. He tried an innocuous one.

"Did you have any trouble finding the cave again?"

"Nay, Bard Pete. Ye little boat which had ta'en us to Ysgard brought Lord Ysgard and me back to ye landing place whence we four had embarked. Thence 'twas a simple matter to retrace ye path back to ye cave. My sense of direction be well developed, ye wist. Here be ye turning. Note that we be making much better time today, sin ye be more experienced in cave-walking."

"I had noticed," said Daniel Stott, who as usual was bringing up the rear. "I must say, however, that I find the experience no more agreeable than heretofore. Also, Medrus, I am somewhat confused by your narrative."

"How so, noble assistant archdruid?"

"Imprimis, you say you had no trouble finding the cave again, and that you knew in advance precisely where Gwrach's hoard was situated. It puzzles me, therefore, that with an efficient ferry service at your disposal, you have not already removed the treasure and made your way back to Ysgard. As we all know, the distance is not so great that you could not have made at least two trips by now in the coracle. Or you might have relied on that excellent sense of direction and brought back packhorses from Lord Ysgard's stable if the hoard is too large to be conveniently removed by boat. Hence, why have you and he elected to remain in the cave so long? I find it hard to credit the possibility that you enjoy being in a situation that occasioned you so much misery in years past."

"Oh well, one getteth used to a place, ye know. In point of

fact, noble sir, Lord Ysgard hath suffered an accident which hath prevented our departure thus far."

"Dear me, how distressing. Why haven't you mentioned it sooner? Is he badly injured?"

"Nay, sire, I cannot say. Belike ye druids, having superior wisdom, will be able to offer an opinion."

"Belike," said Peter somewhat grimly. Medrus still hadn't given a straight answer. He was about to ask for details of Lord Ysgard's accident when the tunnel gave its final wiggle, he saw the reflected flickering of firelight on the walls, and heard a familiar voice pouring out its mournful plaint.

CHAPTER 20

"O waly, waly and welladay me, how I hate to cook. How goeth ye receipt? First catch ye victim. Aye, 'tis done. Disembowel whilst yet breathing. Ugh, how terrible was Gwrach's handwriting. Did she really mean disembowel? Methinks he would soon stop breathing gin I made ye attempt, and then what? 'Twas a bad moment back there when yon scrawny servitor became a raging salamander instead of a disembodied glow because I misread ye words of ye spell. Had he but wist, he could have o'erpowered me at that moment. Then what would have become of poor Dwydd?"

They could see her bent low over a filthy parchment, picking out letters with a clawlike finger, sighing and shaking her head. "Ay me, for my cozy turret and ye banqueting board of ye great and bountiful King Sfyn! Yet here at least be I at last free from ye constant nagging of my wicked niece Edelgysa. Ne'er a letup twixt cockcrow and owl hoot. 'Curse me this one with carbuncles.' 'Put me a murrain on that one.' 'Mix me a potion to effect ye demise of ye other.' I still wish I had put yet another pinch of eye of newt in ye poison for young Prince Dilwyn. He died not peaceful and sudden as befitted his kind and gentle nature, but lingering, with mighty gripes in ye belly, poor lad. And Edelgysa cared not a whit, but rejoiced to have one less prince betwixt her Owain and ye throne. Alas, to be old and at ye mercy of rich relations."

She shoved the parchment aside. "Well, this repining buttereth no parsnips. Gin *Ysgard en daube* be on ye menu tonight, I must e'en puzzle out this disembowelment ere ye guests arrive. 'Tis only correct protocol to feed them ere I kill them. Now that I be mistress in mine own domain, such as it be, it behooveth me to maintain ye standards to which I be accustomed."

Dwydd picked up a large knife and tested the edge on her thumb. " 'Twill do, meseems. 'Tis a loathsome fate I be reduced to, trapping innocent wayfarers to stock my larder. Ne'er yet have I tasted human flesh, and mine own crawleth at ye thought. Almost would I rather starve. But not quite. Innocent wayfarer, I be about to disembowel ye. Wouldst endeavor to keep breathing whilst I hack out thine entrails?"

"Be damned if I will," came the snappish reply. "Hell of a geste this turned out to be, ecod. First I sprain mine ankle and get stuck in this moldy den for three days. Then along cometh an evil hag and turneth mine henchman into some kind of lit-up bug. And now she craveth to slash my guts out. I shall stop breathing any time I take ye notion, hag, and ye can put that in thy pipe and smoke it."

"You tell her, Lord Ysgard," said Peter, stepping forth into the den he remembered so vividly and had hoped never to see again. "Well, Dwydd, I see you've found yourself a new home."

"Aye, and 'twas ye who drove me to it," the crone replied sourly. "I hope ye be satisfied. Making an old woman end her days in a hole in ye ground, instead of my erstwhile comfy quarters at ye castle of King Sfyn."

"Drat it, woman," Peter expostulated, "is it my fault you chose to set yourself up as a witch? Can't you understand you've brought retribution on yourself by brewing up poisons and bashing the edges off swords and kidnapping griffins and maidens and feeding Sir Torchyld that nonsense about being enchanted? What was in those two biscuits you handed him before he went to kill the wyvern, by the way?"

"Naught save henbane, wolfbane, and dogbane," Dwydd answered sullenly. " 'Twas a new receipt I was trying out in ye public interest. I deemed that gin ye wyvern ate Sir Torchyld, it would also swallow ye biscuits and be poisoned, thereby conferring a great boon on ye kingdom of Sfynfford and surrounding realms. Try to perform a kind deed and where doth it get ye?"

"Good question. And this was all your own idea?"

"Nay, dulling ye sword was my wicked niece Edelgysa's doing. I but strove to salvage some good out of her iniquity."

"You're all heart, Dwydd. How did you get to be such great pals with Gwrach?"

" 'Twas but a professional acquaintance, noble bard. My late husband ye wizard summoned her by accident one Beltane eve, and she stayed with us for a spell. Ye see, sire, my husband was not a bad man, but he was in sooth a terrible wizard. At ye end, he became addicted to potions. Morn and night he sat around brewing and swilling and conjuring up satyrs and centaurs to drink with him. Hast ever had to clean up after a parlorful of hairy-hooved debauchers, bard? None wist what I went through ere ye wizard expired in agony from a mismixt elixir. E'en then he left me in parlous state, a lone widow with barely a fillet of fenny snake to my name, not wotting where my next phial of toad sweat was coming from. Bethink ye, I had to pawn my cauldron."

"Gad, yours is a sad tale, madam."

"Ye ha'nt heard ye half of it yet, bard. In mine desperation, I got in touch with Gwrach by a method ye wot of, belike, and begged succor. She scryed an opening for a job at ye castle of King Sfyn, though I misdoubt she and my wicked niece Edelgysa, who by then was wed to ye well-meaning but thick-headed Prince Edwy, had contrived ye vacancy by eliminating ye then resident hag. Gwrach gave me a short course in haggery and taught me ye spell for raising hogweed."

"How did she happen to choose hogweed?"

"La, sire, wist ye not that hogweed be one of ye old standbys in ye wizardly repertoire? Like ye poor, it be always with us, though it lieth dormant in ye soil until ye potent spell be spoke."

"Do tell. And it—er—disappeareth once the spell is unspaken, so to speak?"

"Nay. To vanish ye hogweed, ye must use a special spell, which only I know, methinks, now Gwrach be agone. 'Tis ye only spell I wot how to work, gin ye want ye truth. For aught else I maun rely on potions, trickery, or sleight of hand. And, alas, mine hands be not so sleight as once they were. 'Tis a rotten life for an aging hag.''

A small sigh came from the glow at their feet. "Ay, well do I wot how she feeleth. Poor hag! One might almost feel pity for her, were one's own plight not rendered so dire by her evildoing.''

"M'yes," said Peter. "Now, madam, I gather your position is this. Having been ousted from King Sfyn's castle because of your unholy alliance with Princess Edelgysa, you feel you have no recourse but to take over Gwrach's old stand here and turn mass murderess for a living.''

"Sire, let me clarify my position. I was not ye willing confederate of Gwrach and Edelgysa, but their helpless tool. Gwrach taught me ye spell only on condition that I use ye hogweed to send her victims. Edelgysa got me ye job only so that she could employ me in turn as an instrument of her perfidy. And bitter did I rue my cruel fate.''

"Yet you're quite ready to go on being cruel to line your own stomach.''

"Nay," cried Dwydd. "Methought I could, but I find I cannot. May mine hand wither ere I disembowel this noble lord. Were he but an humble peasant I might bring myself to it, but I have been too long steeped in ye protocol of ye court. 'Tis not ye done thing to show disrespect for one's betters in so gory a manner, and that be ye flat of it. Regard his high, disdainful mien e'en now as I raise ye disemboweling knife. See, he flincheth not when I describe a circle with ye tip of ye blade around his *bogail*.''

"He-he-he," giggled Lord Ysgard. "Get away from my belly button, hag. That tickleth.''

"Aagh!" she cried, flinching back. "He laugheth.''

"So he does," said Peter, "and so do I. Ha-ha to you, silly old woman. Don't you agree, boys? Aren't you laughing, too?''

"Hell, yes," shouted Tim. "Ho-ho-ho.''

"And a lusty guffaw," added Dan Stott, suiting the deed to the word.

That set them all off. Lord Ysgard roared himself red in the face as he adjusted his disarranged garments over the area

Dwydd had laid bare for disemboweling purposes. Peter, Tim, and Dan chortled and pounded each other on the back. Even Medrus ventured a diffident titter. Wondrous to behold, that broke the spell Dwydd had recast upon him. At once he ceased to glimmer and resumed his own unprepossessing shape.

Tim wasn't impressed. "Cripes, Medrus, you looked better as a glow."

"Nay, say not so," cried Dwydd.

She hurled the disemboweling knife into the farthest recesses of the cave and stood before them totally submissive, with tears running down her face, leaving streaks in the dirt.

"With all respect to ye who have ta'en away ye living from a wretched old woman and exposed my once-feared powers for ye shams they be, I find him not uncomely. He remindeth me of my late husband ye wizard, albeit he be sober. He hath that same intellectual brow and ye same scrawny frame. Mark ye well they bags under his eyes. In my husband's case they told of long poring o'er ancient tomes of mystic lore, though I misdoubt this sorry wight hath pored only over ye floor of this accursed cavern."

"Nay," said Medrus, "I be in sooth a man of learning. I can read long words of many letters. I wot to write and cypher. I was clerk to my late liege, Lord Mochyn, ere he fell victim to Gwrach here in this foul den and she made me her vassal e'en as she made this luckless hag."

"That so?" said Lord Ysgard. "I can use a man like ye around ye palace. Gin ye help me carry off yon treasure we came for, ye may stay and work for me. What say ye?"

"I say yes," cried the ex-glow. "Ah, to be a real clerk again, respectably clad in a tunic of reasonably decent quality linen, with a leathern belt around my waist and mine own inkpot depending therefrom. Ah, for ye quill in my hand, ready to inscribe ye words of wisdom that fall from my master's noble lips regarding ye vendage of sheepskins and salted mutton. I may have a tunic, noble master?"

"Aye," said Lord Ysgard, "gin there be any left in Ysgard to fashion ye one. Without women to spin and weave and sew, we be in parlous state."

"There be garments among ye treasure, sire. Gwrach hath stripped them from ye bodies ere she ate her victims. E'en mine own old tunic and inkpot be among them, gin ye rats have left any part uneaten."

"Then, damme, let's go get 'em. I have suffered enow for this vaunted hoard and as yet I see not a groat of it. Er—ye druids be far too holy and unworldly to claim shares, be ye not?"

"Hell, yes," said the archdruid. "It's yours as far as we're concerned. Right, boys?"

"By all means," Daniel Stott confirmed with a gracious inclination of his Jovian head.

"Absolutely," Peter agreed. "You're going to need a little something extra in the old sock, Lord Ysgard. You'll find you've a good many more mouths to feed at home than you had when you left."

"What mean ye?" roared Lord Ysgard. "Have those hot-blooded young devils of mine flouted mine orders? Couldn't wait till I got back, eh? Rode over to Sfynfford armed to ye teeth and abducted themselves a gaggle of princesses, I'll be bound. And now, ecod, I have a war with King Sfyn on my hands, I ween."

"Not at all," Peter assured him. "In the first place, they didn't ride, they went afoot. Prince Yfor very sensibly decided not to take any of your horses away in case some emergency came up while your sons were gone. They left Degwel and your master-at-arms, who seems a capable chap, in charge, and I—er—put a spell on your strong room for the duration of your absence."

"Umph. But ye princesses?"

"No problem there, either. The young ladies were so bowled over by your lads' gallantry that they all fell in love at first sight. The parents could hardly object to such suitable suitors, so they gave consent and threw a first-class wedding. When last seen, the bridal party were all riding back to Ysgard on richly caparisoned chargers, laden with handsome gifts and attended by a number of buxom serving maids."

"Buxom serving maids? Damme, ye don't say! And King Sfyn agreed to ye nuptials?"

"He attended the ceremony in full regalia and gave all six happy couples his official blessing. Also some fine presents, I may add."

"Egad! And my sons bore themselves nobly in ye presence of ye king? Were they dressed as befit their lofty rank?"

"Indeed they were. They'd even had baths. With soap."

"Soap? Be that some magic potion to induce successful husbandry?"

"No, any such potion—er—hardly seemed necessary. Soap is merely a substance used to get dirt off. One applies it in conjunction with water."

"To get dirt off? A quaint and amusing concept, forsooth. Perchance I may try it myself sometime. So I be a father-in-law six times over at one swoop. Be all ye princesses comely of countenance and featly of figure?"

"Your sons certainly appeared to find them attractive."

"Aye, they be chips off ye old block. I don't suppose they thought of bringing one back for their old dad?"

"Sorry, but I'm afraid this time there were only enough princesses to go around. As it happens, however, Princess Aldora, the mother of two of your new daughters-in-law, was widowed under tragic circumstances just as the lads and lasses were plighting their troth. It's possible she might be induced to seek consolation after a suitable period of mourning has elapsed. I expect there's going to be a good deal of visiting back and forth between the palaces."

" 'Twill be my lordly pleasure to wait upon His Majesty with pomp and dignity," said Lord Ysgard, scratching his belly, which must still be tickling from the disemboweling knife. "Now to ye treasure. Lead on, Medrus."

"Right this way, my liege. I humbly regret it be no longer in my power to glow, but we can take brands from ye fire to light ye way."

"Gin I be permitted to accompany ye, I could carry a basket of live embers," Dwydd offered meekly.

"Come ahead, repentant hag. Ye more, ye merrier."

They set off in high fettle, Medrus leading the way, Lord Ysgard at his heels with Dwydd and her coals a respectful three steps behind them. Peter, Tim, and Dan stayed in the rear. They were not much interested in seeing the sorry pile of loot Gwrach had amassed by dint of God knew how many murders. They simply hadn't cared to stay behind in that depressing chamber where they'd had such a gruesome experience with the sow sorceress. Nor were they any too keen on trusting Dwydd, Medrus, or even Lord Ysgard out of their sight until they'd been guided safely away from the cave.

Gwrach had kept her hoard within easy distance of her lair, they were relieved to discover. It was an impressive one, though not a patch on the wyvern's, Peter decided after a quick appraisal. There were few large items like Torchyld's jeweled goblets and golden plates, but many coins and personal items such as chains and finger rings. Also, there were the clothes Medrus had mentioned. Each outfit was encased in a bag evidently spun of cobwebs by trained spiders, to trap the moths and vermin that might otherwise have destroyed the materials. These looked to Peter like obscene cocoons of giant insects, but Medrus fell with joy on the one that contained his own tunic and scribe's gear.

"Ah, now I can be human again."

"And I," said Dwydd, selecting a sober gown of some dark, purplish fabric. "Oh, for a dollop of ye archdruid's soap, that I might cast off my hag's rags and wash myself clean ere donning decent woman's garb."

"As it happens," said Timothy Ames, producing a hornful of his special formula from under his robe, "I brought some with me. Aunt Hilda's lye soap's turned out to be so popular that I figured I might as well keep a little in case it should come in handy on the trip. Go ahead, old woman, have a scrub on me."

"Ecstasy! Ten thousand thanks, noble archdruid. I shall repair to a pool I wot of in one of ye tunnels, and perform mine ablutions."

"And I to another," said Medrus, "gin my liege permitteth, and gin this withered crone I served so briefly yet so faithfully be willing to grant me a share of this intriguing stuff. Ye say it be not for eating?"

"No," Peter explained. "You take some in your hand and moisten it with water so that it makes a lather, then you smear it on your person, rubbing it well into the—er—trouble spots, but being careful to keep it out of your eyes. You then immerse yourself in water and rinse off the soap. The dirt comes off at the same time. It's merely an improvement on the technique you've already—er—been exposed to."

"Ah yes, I grasp ye principle now."

Medrus took his cobweb-wrapped parcel of belongings and headed for his puddle. Dwydd followed suit, modestly choosing a different direction. Lord Ysgard employed their absence gloating over the gold, silver, bronze, and copper, trying to figure out how rich he was going to be. Shandy and his friends leaned up against the cave wall feeling sad and bored, wondering if they were ever going to get the hell out of here again.

They didn't wait long, though. Medrus reappeared in high fettle, looking strangely respectable and clerkly in a brown linen knee-length tunic and leather buskins. He had his inkpot slung from a leather girdle that was somewhat mildewed from the dampness of the cave, but otherwise in good working order. A goose quill pen was stuck behind his right ear.

"Here be I, my liege, ready for work."

"Good man," said Lord Ysgard. "To ye first order of business, then. How be we to carry this treasure out of ye cave?"

"In sacks, my liege. Ye spider webs be uncanny strong. Gwrach empowered ye spiders by a mighty spell she wotted of. Behold."

Medrus had brought his own spider-web sack back with him. He took his little penknife out of the wallet at his waist, slashed the opening at the top wider for easier loading, and began filling the sack with gold and silver.

"Gin ye fill them not too full, they work fine. This be as much as I can carry at a time, anyway. Regard ye."

Medrus swung the sack over his shoulder. As he'd promised, the webbing proved strong enough to hold a reasonable amount of loot. He then began stripping the bags from some of the other pathetically hanging empty garments, and passing them over to be filled. Shandy, Tim, and Dan took a hand, hoping thus to speed their own departure. They were all hard at it when a well-dressed and not uncomely dame appeared, dropping them a low curtsy.

"Great balls of fire," shouted Tim. "Here's the ghost of Ann Boleyn dropping in for tea."

"Can't be," said Peter. "She won't be born for some centuries yet. This, if I'm not mistaken, would be Great-aunt Maud."

"Aye, 'tis Maud," the woman confirmed. "Back in mine proper guise after many a year. A rare old crone I look, meseems."

"Nay," cried Medrus, sidling near. "Ye look—why, Mistress Maud, ye be beautiful!"

She dropped her eyes modestly. "Bethink ye, handsome scribe?"

"Poor varlet hadn't seen a woman in forty years," Lord Ysgard explained in an aside to Daniel Stott. "In sooth, she be none so ill-favored, gin you don't mind 'em a trifle long in ye tooth."

Maud and Medrus didn't hear this observation. They were too wrapped up in each other.

"I believe we are witnessing another case of love at first sight," Daniel Stott observed benignly.

"Then pronounce 'em man and wife and let's get the hell out of here," said Timothy Ames. "Come on, everybody. Grab a sack."

CHAPTER 21

"How much farther do we have to lug these blasted things?" Timothy panted after what seemed like a very long while.

"We should be almost to ye mouth of ye cave," said Medrus, sounding a little worried. "I wot not why we see yet no gleam of daylight or e'en starshine."

"Silly me," gasped his new wife. "I forgot to turn off ye spell. Methinks ye hogweed hath grown around to ye far end of ye cave by now."

Maud was right. When they did get to the opening, they found themselves barricaded by huge, ugly stalks, grunting and groaning and trying to get rootholds in the solid rock.

"Curses," groaned Lord Ysgard. "Foiled again. Now what happeth, former hag? Can ye not get rid of ye stuff somehow?"

"Aye, verily, gin I have thy lordship's solemn promise that I may live at Castle Ysgard with my recently acquired consort Medrus for aye and aye."

"Forsooth, 'tis a big request. I myself be somewhat in ye sere and yellow leaf for any promises about aye and aye. Wouldst settle for a single lifetime? I deem ye might be of some use around ye place, brewing up potions to cure ye flux and drive away mice?"

"Of a surety, sire. I can also banish warts and brew a fool-proof salve for pimples on ye abdomen."

"Then stay and welcome, sobeit ye work no evil spells save at my personal behest gin occasion arise. Doth that satisfy ye?"

"Gramercy, sire. Now do ye stand back and let me see gin I can still work ye hogweed spell."

Maud rolled up her sleeves, wove her hands together with the fingers interlocking, the palms facing out and the thumbs pointing down. She began to revolve slowly widdershins, chanting in a low monotone, "Ring around a rosy. **Begone,** disgusting posy. Hogweed, hogweed, all fall down."

"That's all you're going to do?" Peter demanded incredulously.

He'd hardly got the words out of his mouth when the hogweed collapsed with a resounding whoosh, and the way was cleared.

"I'll be damned."

He set down the sack he'd been carrying and stepped out onto the stalks. They felt strangely flat, almost like a wooden floor. And the air smelled strange, not like the cave nor yet like the outdoors. He could swear it smelled of beer.

It did. There stood the bar with nobody behind it. There glittered the brass pump handles. And here came Timothy Ames and Daniel Stott.

"Sorry to have taken so long, Pete," said Tim. "We've been talking to the publican. He'll be in as soon as he gets some firewood. He tells us there's an inn just around the bend where we can put up for the night and get a pretty decent meal."

"Fine," Peter answered. "When he comes, ask him to draw me a pint of bitter, will you? I think I'll just step out for a minute and take a look at that hogweed before the light goes."

It was ridiculous, no doubt. Quite as silly as the serpent with its tail in its mouth that turned into the DNA molecule, or the flowers in Einstein's garden murmuring sweetly, "$E = MC^2$." He walked down behind the parking lot wall, linked his fingers outward with the thumbs pointing down, and revolved his body counterclockwise.

"Ring around a rosy. Begone, disgusting posy. Hogweed, hogweed, all fall down."

The leaves didn't even quiver. Peter shrugged, turned, and walked back to get his pint. He was about halfway to the pub's door when he heard a mighty swish behind him.

It was a sound Peter remembered well from his childhood, of cornstalks falling behind the slash of his grandfather Shandy's well-sharpened scythe after the ears had been gathered and it was time to put the fodder in the shock. He went in, drank his pint, and treated the boys to another round. Then he put in a phone call to his wife, but got no answer. She and Iduna must still be out sight-seeing.

He didn't manage to reach Helen until some time later, after he, Dan, and Tim had dined on excellent spring lamb and fresh green peas, with strawberries and cream for afters. She sounded happy to hear from him, though.

"Hello, darling. I have a million things to tell you, so I'd better give you this message before I forget. Some professor from the university with a name like Pfylltrydd's been trying to get hold of you. He wants you to call him back right away."

Helen gave him a number, then went on to tell of her and Iduna's doings. Peter let her talk until she ran out of steam, thinking how delightfully sane she sounded. Then he assured her he was fine.

"No, just a little tired, that's all. It's been a long day. I expect we'll be back tomorrow, though. And damned glad of it. Sleep well."

He hung up, checked out the number he'd written down, and rang Pfylltrydd. The professor himself answered.

"Ah, Professor Shandy, I'm so glad I've managed to contact you. It seems a rather extraordinary thing is happening. We're suddenly getting floods of reports about the hogweed."

"Really?" said Peter. "What are they saying?"

"You may not credit this, but the plants are wilting. Quite without warning. They just flop over and die."

"M'yes, I must say I've been expecting something of the sort. Sooner or later, the stuff grows too tall to sustain its own weight. The bigger they are, the harder they fall, you know. I shouldn't be surprised if the hogweed's all gone in a day or so. Make a bit of a stink when it rots, but that shouldn't last long enough to be any great problem. So you won't be needing me and my colleagues, after all."

"Quite to the contrary, Professor Shandy. According to my information, a 'Save the Giant Hogweed' movement is already being formed, and a seminar is being planned for Thursday week. I've already been asked to speak, and I was hoping you could favor us with a few words, also."

"Sorry," said Peter, "but my wife has other plans for me.

You might tell your group to simmer down. From what Professor Ames, Professor Stott, and I have gathered so far, we're inclined to believe *Heracleum mantegazzianum* is—er—cyclical in nature, like bamboo, only—er—more so. It will pop up again, sooner or later. Just remind them for me, there'll always be a hogweed."

Very, very gently, Peter Shandy hung up the phone and went to bed.

ABOUT THE AUTHOR

Charlotte MacLeod, who lives in Massachusetts, is the author of many books, short stories, and articles for adults and children. She has published nine previous novels in the Crime Club, including four other Peter Shandy stories: *Rest You Merry, The Luck Runs Out, Wrack and Rune,* and *Something the Cat Dragged In.*